Clan MacLean

The Clan MacLean

Instituted 1892

Clan MacLean

The Clan MacLean
Instituted 1892

ISBN/EAN: 9783337392321

Printed in Europe, USA, Canada, Australia, Japan

Cover: Foto ©Andreas Hilbeck / pixelio.de

More available books at **www.hansebooks.com**

INSTITUTED 1892.

PRICE ONE SHILLING.

GLASGOW :
JOHN THOMLINSON, Stanley Works, Partick.
1893.

CONSTITUTION AND RULES.

I.—The Association shall be called "THE CLAN MACLEAN."

II.—The objects of the Association shall be the reviving, fostering, and promoting of Clan interests and sentiments, by collecting and preserving records and traditions in any way relating to the Clan; the cultivation of social intercourse among the Members; the rendering of assistance to necessitous and deserving Clansmen and Clanswomen; the encouraging of the study of the Gaelic language and literature, and education generally.

III.—The membership shall consist of Life, Extraordinary, and Ordinary Members. Life Members shall contribute a single payment of not less than Three Guineas; Extraordinary Members an annual subscription of not less than Ten Shillings and Sixpence; and Ordinary Members an annual subscription of not less than Two Shillings and Sixpence. Ladies, an annual subscription of not less than One Shilling; and those residing in rural districts of the Highlands and Islands of Scotland, or serving as non-commissioned Officers or Privates in Her Majesty's Army, or as Seamen in the Royal Navy, shall contribute an annual subscription of not less than One Shilling. Ladies can become Life Members by contributing a single payment of not less than one guinea.

IV.—All persons bearing the surname MACLEAN in any of its various forms or spellings, including ladies, bearing the name either by parentage or by marriage, shall be eligible as Members; also, persons bearing other surnames, but whose maternal parent was a MACLEAN, are eligible as Members, but not as Office-Bearers.

V.—The Office-Bearers of the Association shall consist of the Hereditary Chief and Chieftains of the Clan, a President, six Vice-Presidents, a Council, consisting of not less than six nor more than twenty Members; a Treasurer or Joint Treasurers, and a Secretary or Joint Secretaries, who shall constitute a Council of Management, and who, with the exception of the Hereditary Chief, shall be elected annually at the General Meeting of the Association.

The Hereditary Chief and Chieftains shall hold office for life.

VI.—The Funds of the Association shall be lodged in a Bank in Glasgow, in name of the CLAN MACLEAN Association, and the said account shall be operated upon by Cheques drawn by

the Treasurer, and signed by the Secretary and President, or any of the Vice-Presidents.

VII.—The Ordinary Meetings of the Association in Glasgow shall be held on the first Thursday of each Month, from October to April inclusive. The Meeting in April shall be the Annual General Meeting, at which a Statement of Intromissions, signed by one or more Auditors, showing the state of the Association's affairs during the preceding year, shall be submitted, and on approval shall be engrossed in the sederunt book of the Association.

VIII.—No addition to, or alteration of, the constitution shall be made, except at the Annual General Meeting of the Association by the resolution of two-thirds of the Members present. Notice of such addition or alteration shall be given in writing to the Secretary one calendar month prior to the date of said meeting, and shall be specified by him in the intimation calling the meeting, at which the same is to be discussed.

BRANCH RULES.

I.—A Branch of the CLAN MACLEAN Association may be formed in any district containing Twenty Members, and such Branch shall be subject in every respect to the Constitution and Rules of the Association.

II.—Each Branch shall be managed by a Chairman, Vice-Chairman, and not more than seven Members of Committee,—two of whom shall be the Treasurer and the Secretary. Each Branch shall have the right to appoint its own Office-Bearers.

III.—The Treasurer shall receive all subscriptions and donations, and shall enter regularly in a book kept for the purpose an account of all monies received and paid by him for ordinary local expenses. He shall make up such accounts to the 31st October and 31st March respectively, and shall within seven days thereafter send to the Secretary of the Association a copy of such accounts, duly vouched and audited, together with a remittance of the cash on hand. All accounts shall be subject to the final approval of the Council. He shall not at any time retain in his hands more than three pounds.

IV.—Each Branch Secretary shall conduct all correspondence, keep proper books, and other records of all Branch transactions and meetings, and prepare a report annually, which after being approved at a meeting of the Branch Committee, shall be forwarded to the Secretary of the Association, at least twelve days prior to the Annual General Meeting of the Association.

V.—The Council reserve power to alter the above Rules as they may see fit.

Clan MacLean Association.

INSTITUTED 1892.

OFFICE-BEARERS FOR 1893-94.

Chief.

Col. Sir Fitzroy Donald MacLean, Bart. of Duart, Morvern
and Brolas.

Chieftains.

MacLean of Gailean (Swedish Branch).
MacLean of Pennycross.
MacLean of Torloisk.
MacLean of Ardgour.

President.

R. MacLean MacLean, Eliot Hill, Kent.

Chaplain.

The Rev. John MacLean, D.D., 189 Hill Street, Glasgow.

Vice-Presidents.

Magnus MacLean, M.A., F.R.S.E., 8 St. Albans Ter., Glasgow.
John MacLean, 60 Mitchell Street, Glasgow.
William MacLean, 115 St. Vincent Street, Glasgow.
A. H. MacLean, Hughenden Terrace, Kelvinside, Glasgow.
Lachlan M'Lean, 68 St. Vincent Crescent, Glasgow.
William MacLean, 58 West George Street, Glasgow.

Treasurer.

C. J. MacLean, Writer, 115 St. Vincent Street, Glasgow.

Joint Treasurer.

A. J. MacLean, 73 Byres Road, Partick, Glasgow.

Secretary.

John MacLean, 73 Byres Road, Partick, Glasgow.

Councillors.

Archibald MacLean, 149 Renfrew Street, Glasgow.
Neil MacLaine, 2 Rutland Crescent, Paisley Road, Glasgow.
Robert MacLean, 31 Cadogan Street, Glasgow.
Donald MacLean, 40 South Portland Street, Glasgow.

JOHN MACLEAN, 86 Wilson Street, Glasgow.
DR. MACLEAN, 88 Paisley Road, Glasgow.
ALLAN S. MACLEAN, 78 George Street, Whiteinch, Glasgow.
WILLIAM Q. MACLEAN, 36 Dumbarton Road, Partick, Glasgow.
DUNCAN MACLEAN, 40 Edmund Street, Dennistoun, Glasgow.
JOHN MACLEAN, 100 Barrack Street, Glasgow.
DONALD MACLEAN, 296 Buchanan Street, Glasgow.
SPENCER B. MACLEAN, Woodlands Road, Glasgow.
DONALD MACLEAN, 15 MacLean Street, Plantation, Glasgow.
HECTOR MACLEAN, 34 Blantyre Street, Glasgow.
JOHN MACLEAN, 73 North Street, Glasgow.
HUGH MACLEAN, 310 Garscube Road, Glasgow.
JOHN MACLEAN, 4 Buchanan Street, Partick, Glasgow.
PETER MACLEAN, 76 Elderslie Street, Glasgow.
CHARLES MACLEAN, 3 Cadzow Street, Anderston, Glasgow.

Clan Piper.

WILLIAM MACLEAN, 4 Trafalgar Street, Greenock.

Clan Bard.

JOHN MACLEAN, Ballymartin, Tiree.

GREENOCK BRANCH.

President.

ARCHIBALD MACLEAN, 4 Trafalgar Street, Greenock.

Secretary.

DUGALD MACLEAN, 19 Hamilton Street, Greenock.

District Secretaries.

PETER MACLEAN, Solicitor, Lochmaddy.
EWEN MACLEAN, 112 Church Street, Inverness.
COLIN MACLEAN, Mid Dana, Knapdale.
ANGUS MACLEAN, Scrap, Tarbert, Harris.
MALCOLM MACLEAN, Kirkpool, Tiree.
Rev. ARTHUR JOHN MACLEAN, Dean of Argyle & the Isles, Portree.
PETER MACLEAN, Forester, Invergarry.
WILLIAM MACLEAN, Mishnish Hotel, Tobermory.
MURDO MACLEAN, Lochbroom, Ross-shire.
C. A. MACLEAN, Writer, Wigton.
ALLAN MACLEAN, 62 Alexandria Street, Alexandria.
REV. F. MACLEAN, Banff.
J. A. MACLEAN, Union Bank House, Forfar.
A. MACLEAN, 115 Main Street, Bradford, U.S.A.
C. H. MACLEAN, Fintry, Aberdeen.
DUNCAN MACLEAN, 13 Alexandria Grove, Manchester.
JOHN W. MACLEAN, 42-44 State Street, Chicago.
LACHLAN MACLEAN, Kinloch, Pennyghael, Mull.

FIRST ANNUAL GATHERING.

Held in Glasgow, 28th October, 1892.

The following account of the First Annual Gathering is taken from the *Oban Times*, of 5th November, 1892 :—

THE CLAN MACLEAN.

Last Friday evening the First Annual Gathering of the Clan MacLean was held in the Grand Hall, Waterloo Rooms. There was a large attendance, presided over by the chief of the Clan, Sir Fitzroy Donald MacLean, Bart. of Duart, Morvern, and Brolas, who was accompanied by Sir Andrew MacLean, Partick ; Rev. John MacLean, D.D. ; ex-Provost MacLean, Govan ; Mr. Magnus MacLean, M.A., Glasgow ; Mr. and Mrs. MacLean, Pennycross ; C. J. MacLean, treasurer, Mrs. C. J. MacLean, Professor Blackie, Rev. Jas. MacLean, Mrs. and Miss MacLean, Mr. J. MacLean, secretary ; Mr. Wm. MacLean, writer ; Mr. A. MacLean, Mr. Peter MacLean, solicitor, Lochmaddy ; Dr. C. R. MacLean, Dennistoun ; Messrs. Arch. MacLean, president ; and Dugald MacLean, secretary, Greenock Branch ; besides representatives from the various clan societies. Letters of apology were intimated from MacLean, Torloisk ; MacLean, Ardgour ; Lord Compton, M.P. ; Surgeon General MacLean, Thurso ; John MacLean, Clan Bard, Tiree ; Mr. Donald M'Millan, vice-president, Clan MacMillan, &c. During the assembling of the audience the Clan pipers played selections of pipe-music. After tea,

The Chairman, who was loudly cheered, said :—Clansmen, ladies and gentlemen,—It is with the greatest possible gratification that I feel myself able to take part in the very interesting occasion which has brought us together this evening, and when I look at the very large assemblage before me, and note the cordial welcome you have given, I cannot fail to realise that the lapse of a century and a half does not cause MacLeans either to forget the noble traditions of their ancestors, or the hereditary chief of their Clan. (Cheers.) Ladies and gentlemen, I thank you most sincerely for for your kind reception of me, and for the great honour you have conferred upon me by placing me in the chair. (Applause.) As chairman it would be my pleasing duty to bring before you various subjects in connection with the Clan Society, but with your permission I will ask the president of the committee to do so, and will confine myself to one or two remarks. The heads of the leading houses have been elected office-bearers, and we may rest assured that the honour of the Clan is in safe keeping in the hands of the president, six vice-presidents, the councillors, and

members. (Cheers.) The rules have been drawn out with every care, and I trust to your satisfaction. We are all very well pleased to welcome our clansmen from the Greenock Branch. Ere long we hope a Clan Society will be established in London. (Hear, hear.) Other branches will probably be formed. We have many true and loyal clansmen in Canada and the United States, and I have great pleasure in naming the Rev. A. MacLean Sinclair, and Professor J. P. MacLean, the former being a great authority on Highland and Gaelic literature, and to the latter we are indebted for a most interesting history of the Clan. (Applause.) When I visited the new world I found the name MacLean everywhere respected, and their loyalty to their chief most marked. (Applause.) We are honoured this evening by the presence of several distinguished members of the Clan. Many are well known to you, and reside on the soil so much beloved by them—Pennycross, Kinlochaline, Torloisk. We heartily welcome the Counts MacLean of Sweden, who enobled their name after they settled in that country, and were held in the highest esteem. I was present at an interview with the King of Sweden at Christiania, and heard his Majesty's courteous remarks respecting them. (Applause.) The head of the following houses sent their regrets at being unable to be present :—The Marquis of Northampton ; Ardgour, owing to his youth, could not attend; my eldest son, Hector, is preparing for an examination or he would have been present ; and Lady MacLean deeply regrets not being well enough to attend, but hopes to do so on another occasion, and begs you will accept her apologies. (Cheers.) I am confident my clansmen will agree with me that we may be congratulated on having in our ranks Sir Andrew MacLean, who, through, his own merits, has not only gained the highest position among the citizens of this great and important City, but has received the honour of knighthood from Her Gracious Majesty. (Cheers.) Then we have our learned and esteemed friend of many years standing, Professor Blackie, who is always welcome. (Applause.) Equally welcome are the members of other clans and associations, especially those who belong to the Mull and Iona Association, of which I have the honour to be president. (Hear, hear.) A short time ago I visited the battlefield of Harlaw—fought, as you know, on the 24th July, 1411. I was at once shown the spot where Sir Hector MacLean of Duart, and Sir Alexander Irvine of Drum slew each other in combat. Their bravery has never been forgotten to this day. (Cheers.) No one can read the account of the behaviour of the Clan at Glenlivet on 3rd October, 1594, under Sir Lauchlan MacLean, without feelings of pride. At Inverkeithing, on 20th July, 1551, our battle cry, "Fear eile air son Eachainn," was heard to some purpose, and I now hold in my hand the list of killed and wounded. Their brave names shall be heard by all

present, and your hearts will know how to receive them, viz :—
List of killed and wounded, Clan MacLean.—Killed—Sir Hector
MacLean of Duart and Morven, colonel of foot for the County of
Argyle—chief of the Clan MacLean ; Lachlan, son of MacLean of
Torloisk ; John and Donald, sons of MacLean of Ardgour ; Hugh,
Murdoch, and Allan, of Coll, sons of Lachlan Abhar MacLean ;
Lachlan, Ewen, and John, of Ardnacroish, MacLeans of Ross,
race of the Iron Sword ; Hugh, son of MacLean of Isle of Muck ;
Allan, son of MacLean of Drimnin ; Archibald, son of MacLean
of Borreray ; Charles, son of MacLean of Inverscaddle. Severely
wounded—Donald MacLean of Brolas, uncle of the chief,
lieut.-col. commandant of Clan MacLean ; John MacLean of
Kinlochetive ; Ewen MacLean of Treshnish, the gallant captain
of Cairnberg ; John of Totronald, son of MacLean of Coll ; John
Diurach MacLean of Ardtornish ; Neil MacLean of Drumnacross.
Strength, 800 ; killed, 760 ; survived, 40 ; race of the Iron Sword
lost, 140. We do not forget Killiecrankie (1689), nor that our
Clan followed the great Montrose, and shared all his triumphs.
(Applause.) Clansmen, go to St. Giles' Cathedral, and it will be
with feetings of pride that you see the arms of their chief,
MacLean of Duart, who commanded the Clan, overhanging the
beautiful monument erected to the memory of that brave man.
(Cheers.) Alas ! we come to the 16th April, 1746. The Clan
MacLean mustered not far from Inverness, and numbered 500.
They were poorly clad, indifferently equipped, and so badly
provided with food that many wandered the greater part of the
previous night to get what they could to prevent starvation. The
gathering sounded, and shortly the Highlanders found the enemy
on Culloden Moor. On the MacLean left were the Clanranald,
Keppoch, and Glengarry clans, all under the Duke of Perth.
The order was given to advance. The MacLeans rushed forward,
attacked the Duke of Cumberland's right flank, and though they
fought like lions they were unsupported and obliged to retire.
(Applause.) The whole of the front rank, chiefly composed of
gentlemen of the Clan, was swept away. All the leaders were
killed, including the brave MacLean of Drimnin. That was the
last gathering of the Clan until this evening. Under the happy
rule of our gracious Queen—God bless her !—we live in peaceful
times, and I have not to raise the "Fiery Cross," nor ask
you to arm yourselves with all the weapons you can find,
but I do call upon you, as your chief, to arm yourselves
with manly determination to uphold the honour of this noble
Clan, and never to forget the name you bear wherever your
path in life may lead you ; face its dangers and troubles with the
courage of your ancestors, and you will succeed. (Loud cheers.)

Professor Blackie, in addressing the meeting, said that he was
not a Highlander. He had no Highland blood in his veins. He

B

was born in Charlotte Street, Glasgow, not in the west end—laughter—83 years ago, and he was simply a Scotchman who loved the Highlands and Highlanders. (Applause). He had visited the Highland glens, and saw nothing but desolation in the land. The landlords had in too many cases behaved in a scandalous manner, being content to hand over their estates to the management of factors, who collected the rents which the lairds were so anxious to spend in London. For saying such things he had drawn down upon him the hatred of those who had been guilty of such conduct—but he did'nt care, for he did what was right, and he had earned the gratitude and love of the Highlanders. (Applause.) It was the duty of the lairds to learn the language of the people, and take a deeper interest in their welfare than they had done in the past. It had been truly said—"The way to a mother's heart is through her children; the way to a people's heart is through its language." It was this that made him study Gaelic. He would advise them to love their country and their language, act naturally, and believe in themselves rather than allow themselves to be swallowed up by the omnivorous John Bull.. (Applause.) Why should they not prefer their own Gaelic songs to those of any nation? (Applause.)

Towards the close of the proceedings, the Rev. John MacLean, D.D., addressed the meeting. He said he looked upon the meeting as a large family party. It was certainly the largest gathering of the Clan he had ever witnessed. (Applause.) He rejoiced to see them meeting as a Clan for the furtherance of objects which were truly excellent. (Applause.) Of course, he was aware that in commending the formation of a Clan Society he would be blamed by the philosopher and the theologian. The former believed in cosmopolitanism. That was a long word, and it was a sign of the weakness of his cause when he had to go so far afield to find a word to express his meaning. (Laughter.) Let them try as they might they could not get rid of the family idea associated with the Clan. Why should they be ashamed of being called a clannish people? When they heard of a brave deed done they were always better pleased to find that it had been done by a clansman than by a member of any other clan. (Applause.) He shared that sentiment to a large extent. (Applause.) Of course, very many foolish and bad things had been done under the clan system, but they were not seeking to restore that system in all its details, even if that were possible. What they aimed at was to conserve what was best in the clan system, and upon this basis to build a superstructure that would be creditable to them as a Clan and worthy of the age in which they lived. (Applause.) Although living far from the scenes of the early history of the Clan, they could ever aim at making theirs the model Clan, and in this way they would be doing greater good

than was probably ever done in the past by the Clan. They could illustrate in their life and conduct what the clan system was capable of being made in the Nineteenth Century. (Applause.) Were they to keep alive the best traits of the clan system, there was nothing to prevent their carrying the clan banner aloft, and making the name of the Clan as honoured as ever it was. (Applause.) If they acted worthy of their traditions as a Clan, the clan system would be honoured, and would have a good effect on the branch of the nation to which they belonged. (Applause.) The clan system was best suited to their nature, and they might rest assured that more good was likely to result from the carrying out of the family or clan idea than by the attempt to found a universal brotherhood, which was far beyond their capacity. (Loud applause.)

Provost MacLean, Govan, proposed a vote of thanks to their Chief for his kindness in coming to preside over them that evening. (Applause.)

The gallant Chairman, in acknowledging the compliment said—I am sorry we have to part so soon. I thank you for your kindness in giving me attention, and I will only add a few more words before we part, for we know not when we shall meet again; but, believe me, there is a cord which unites the heart of your chief with those of the children of his tribe which neither absence, vicissitude, nor success can rend asunder. (Hear, hear.) I am very proud of my Clan, and of the honour of wearing three eagle's plumes in my bonnet, and I trust.I may ever be deserving of your confidence, your attachment, and your affection. That any action of mine should be approved of by my clansmen is sufficient and the greatest reward I could desire. (Cheers.)

The singing of "Auld Lang Syne" terminated a most successful concert.

A successful assembly followed the concert,—the grand march being led by the gallant chairman and Mrs. MacLean, Pennycross.

MACLEAN BARDS[*]

BY

Magnus MacLean, M.A.

Although I have attempted to write a paper on "MacLean Bards," I cannot pretend to have any special qualifications for such an arduous task. The subject is a wide one, and it would require the spending of a great deal of time and labour to make the paper anything like complete and satisfactory. As I could only spend odd moments, snatched at intervals from my own proper sphere of studies, no doubt many names that ought to have been included are omitted. I shall be grateful if any member will send me the name and songs of any other Clan Bards. Nevertheless, the list I have compiled is a formidable one—one that will undoubtedly surprise many, even members of the Clan. In the collation of them I have received invaluable help from the works of Rev. A. MacLean Sinclair, Prince Edward Island, a gentleman who has done much in the field of Gaelic literature, especially in publishing Gaelic songs, which otherwise might have been lost to posterity. It would have been comparatively easy to write a popular essay on the subject I have chosen, one that would be more interesting and enjoyable to you to-night, than the one I have written; but my object was to draw attention to as many as I could find of MacLean Bards, and to say but little on each in this paper, in the hope that some one of yourselves would take up one or more of them in greater detail some other night before this Clan MacLean Association.

Perhaps it would not be out of place for me to read the following extract from a letter I received from Rev. A. MacLean Sinclair in November last :—

"I see by the *Oban Telegraph* that the Clan MacLean Society was to have a meeting on the 28th of October. I rejoice very much that such a society has been formed. It was greatly needed. There are several historic points to be cleared up. The MacLeans have reason to be proud of their history. I hope they will all take an interest in the work of the Society. I would like to know something about the nature and working of the Society. I presume the main work is not to meet and eat and talk, but to collect all possible facts about the Clan and the branches and members of it.

---

[*] Read before the Clan MacLean Association, Glasgow, 6th January, 1893.

If I were a MacLean I would gladly join it, but I am not. I take
for granted that you will publish all the historic papers that may be
read before your Society. If so, perhaps you will let me have the
opportunity of being a subscriber for them. I would like to get
them."

The following is a list of the MacLean Bards, so far as I have
been able to collate them from the materials at my disposal :—

MACLEAN BARDS.

Hector MacLean, An Cleireach Beag, Coll, 1537.
Hector MacLean, Eachunn Bacach, Mull, 1651.
Captain Andrew MacLean of Knock, Anndra mac an Easbuig,
    Mull, 1635.
Catherine MacLean, Catriona nighean Eoghain mhic Lachuinn,
    born 1650, Coll.
Lachlan MacLean, Lachunn mac mhic Iain, Coll, 1687.
John MacLean, Iain mac Ailein, Mull, 1665 to 1760.
Donald Ban MacLean, Mull, 1715.
Margaret MacLean, Maircread nighean Lachuinn mhic Iain,
    1700-1750.
Rev. John MacLean, Mull, died 1756.
An t-Aireach Muileach : *See "Gaelic Bards" by MacLean Sinclair,
    page 159.*
Iain mac Thearlaich Oig, Inverscadel, 1745.
Eoghain Mac-Ghilleain am Barra.
Malcolm MacLean, Calum a Ghlinne, Kinlochewe, Ross-shire,
    died 1764.
Archibald MacLean, Gilleasbuig Laidir, Tiree, died 1830.
Donald MacLean, Domhnull Bàn na Libe, Mull, died about 1830.
Alexander MacLean, An Cubair Colach, went to Australia, 1840.
Rev. Duncan MacLean, Glenorchy, born 1796, died 1871.
John MacLean, Am Bard Mac Ghilleain, Tiree and Canada,
    1787 to 1848.
Donald MacLean, Domhnull Cubair, brother to John the Poet,
    1770 to 1868.
Charles MacLean, son of John the Poet, 1813 to 1880.
Lachlan MacLean, Lachunn na' mogan, Coll and Glasgow, 1799
    to 1845.
John MacLean, Waternish, Skye, died 1878.
John MacLean, Tiree, Manitoba.
Alexander MacLean, Alastair Mor, Tiree, died 15 years ago
Rev. Alex. Thomson MacLean, Baillieston, 1832 to 1882.
Rev. Hector MacLean, Lochalsh : *Gael. Vol. III.*
William MacLean of Plantation, 1805 to 1892.
J. C. MacLean, Glasgow, 1843.
Hector MacLean, Eachunn Ruadh, Tobermory, Mull.
Lachlan MacLean, Lachunn Eli, Mull, died 1882.

Charles MacLean, Aird Meadhonach, Mull, died 1890.
Janet MacLean (Biog), Coll.

Living Poets.

John MacLean, Ballymartin, Tiree, Bard to the Association.
Andrew MacLean, Kenton, 1848—Brooklyn.
Duncan MacLean, Dunoon and Manchester.
Hugh Archibald MacLean, Dunoon and Manchester.
Neil MacLaine, Tiree and Glasgow.
John MacLean, grand-nephew of John the Poet, Tiree.
John MacLean, Iain mac Dhomhnuill mhic Eachuinn.
John MacLean, Iain mac Iain mhic Eachuinn.
Peter MacLean, Largs and Glasgow.
Maggie MacLean, Dunvegan, Skye.
Neil MacLean, Creig, Mull.
Lachlan MacLean, Lachunn Neill, Muck and Oban.
James MacLean, son to Lachlan, Milngavie.
Mary MacLean, grand-daughter of John the Poet, Franklin.

AN CLEIREACH BEAG.

Hector MacLean, fourth Laird of Coll, known as " An Cleireach
Beag," lived in the middle of the sixteenth century. He was a
good man, an excellent scholar, and a first-rate poet. Many of
his songs were composed in Latin. Allan MacLean, son of
Lachlann Catanach MacLean of Duart, was then the scourge of
the West Highlands. He had a small fleet under his command,
by means of which he made plundering excursions to many parts,
and several chiefs bought immunity by giving him presents of
lands and castles. In this way he got possession of Gigha and
Tarbert Castle. He is better known as "Ailein nan Sop," and it
is said that he was named thus, because he frequently set wisps of
burning straw to the houses which he had first plundered. The
Laird of Coll being highly displeased at Allan's conduct in this
respect composed a song greatly to his disparagement. As soon
as Allan heard of it, he at once proceeded to Coll, seized the
"Cleireach Beag," and confined him as a prisoner in Tarbert
Castle. It was while Hector MacLean was here that he composed
"Caismeachd Ailein nan Sop." Allan was so pleased with the
tenor of this song, that he immediately gave his liberty to the
author. This would be about 1537.

EACHUNN BACACH.

Hector MacLean lived in the beginning of the seventeenth
century. It is said that he was present at the battle of Inverkeithing, July 20, 1651, along with eight brothers who were all
killed. He himself received a wound from which he was lame
ever afterwards, and hence he is commonly known as Eachunn

.

Bacach. He was poet to Sir Lachlan MacLean of Duart, from whom he had a small annuity, and in praise of whom the bard composed several songs. Three of his songs are published in " Beauties of Gaelic Poetry," and Rev. A. MacLean Sinclair has published several others in " Clarsach na Coille," and in " The Gaelic Bards from 1411 to 1765." To most of the songs given in " The Gaelic Bards," valuable historical notes are added by Mr. MacLean Sinclair.

ANNDRA MAC AN EASBUIG.

Captain Andrew MacLean of Knock, Bishop Hector's eldest son, or as he is better known, Anndra mac-an-Easbuig, was born about the year 1535. He entered the army, rose to the rank of captain, retired, and lived the rest of his days in Mull. He composed several very good songs, the best known being "Oran Gaoil, to Barbara, daughter of Bishop Fullarton," and the " Iorram" he composed shortly after the death of his own wife and the death of his two brothers, Sir Alexander and Captain John, the former of whom died at Aix-La-Chapelle, and the latter was killed at Reyzerwerts.

In 1704, the learned Edward Lhuyd of Wales published his " Archæologia Britannica," which contained a Gaelic-English vocabulary. The second edition of this work appeared in 1707, and in it were inserted complimentary poetical addresses by several Highlanders. The first is by Captain Andrew MacLean of Knock, and the following may be taken as a free translation of it :—

> Excellent is thy work completed ;
> Thy deep lore is widely known ;
> The sweet language of our fathers
> Grandly to the world hast shown.
> Praise shall be of Lhuyd's great labours,
> Which henceforth we emulate ;
> Friendship for the Gael of England
> In our hearts he does create.

CATRIONA NIGHEAN EOGHAIN MHIC LACHUINN.

Catherine MacLean, or Catriona nighean Eoghain mhic Lachuinn belonged to Coll, and seems to have been contemporary with Lachlan MacLean. At any rate we find her composing a *cumha* to Triath Cholla (Lachlan MacLean).

> Gu bheil maithean na duthcha
> Fo throm churam an drasta,
> Mo'n uachdaran chliuiteach
> Marcaich ur nan steud arda,
> Chaidh thu tamull do dh·Eirinn
> Do 'n Eiphit 's do 'n Spain,
> 'S nuair chaidh thu do Lunnain
> Fhuair thu 'n t·urram thar chach.

Cait an robh ann an Albainn
Beachd meanmna mo ruin ?
Laoch gasta, deas, dealbhach,
'S tric a dhearbh thu do chliu.
Corp bu ghile na maghar
Bha fo 'n aghaidh gun smur ;
'Se fhag mise fo leatrom
Am ball seirce 'bha 'd ghnuis.

She composed many other songs, mostly to the Coll MacLeans or
their relations. All her songs show much tenderness of feeling,
and high poetic power.

LACHUNN MAC-MHIC IAIN.

We know very little of Lachlan MacLean, or Lachunn Mac-
Mhic Iain, except that he was descendant of the MacLeans of
Coll, probably a grandson of John Garbh MacLean, seventh of
Coll. He composed several very good songs. The cumha to
Lachlunn Mac Ghilleain, Triath Cholla, *a bhathadh 's a' bliadhna*,
1687, has great merit.

Marbhaisg air an t-saoghal chruaidh
'S laidir buan an cairich' e ;
Cha 'n 'eil mionaid ann san uair,
Nach bi ghluasad mearachdach ;
Aig feobhas 's a bhios a sgeimh
Bheir luchd-bleid an aire dha ;
'S gun d' aithnich mis'orm fein
Gum bu bhreug a gheallaidhean.

An ni sin shaoileas tu bhi 'd laimh,
'Se gun dail gun mhearachd ann
Ma 's ni glaiste san tigh stoir
Ge b'e or no eallach e,
No duine mascullach og
'San cuir thu dochas barantais
Sud e seachad mar am fiar
'S ochain ! threig mo bharail mi.

IAIN MAC AILEIN.

John MacLean, better known as Iain Mac Ailein, or Iain mac
Ailein mhic Iain mhic Eoghain, is entitled to a high place, not only
among the MacLean Bards, but among the Bards of the Highlands
and Islands generally. He belonged to the Ardgour branch of
the MacLeans ; being indeed the great grandson of Eoghan na
h-Iteige, who was the sixth MacLean of Ardgour. The poet lived all
his days in Mull, namely, from 1665 till about 1745. Rev. Nigel
MacNeill in his " Literature of the Highlanders " gives 1760 as the
date of his death. I may quote you the references made to this
poet, both in Boswell's Tour and Johnson's own Tour to the
Western Islands. When they arrived in Mull, they called on
Dr. Hector MacLean, who took down the poet's songs, and who
is represented by Boswell as having written a History of the
MacLeans.

Dr. Hector MacLean was not at home when they called, but his daughter entertained them so well that Dr. Johnson says of her next morning, "She is the most accomplished lady that I have found in the Highlands. She knows French, music, and drawing, sews neatly, makes shell-work, and can milk cows; in short, she can do everything. She talks sensibly, and is the first person whom I have found that can translate Erse poetry literally."

This is Boswell's account of their reception by Miss MacLean. "Miss MacLean produced some Erse poems by John MacLean, who was a famous bard in Mull, and had died only a few years ago. He could neither read nor write. She read and translated two of them; one a kind of elegy on Sir John MacLean's being obliged to fly his country in 1715; another a dialogue between two Roman Catholic young ladies, sisters, whether it was better to be a nun or to marry. I could not perceive much poetical imagery in the translation. Yet all of our company who understood Erse seemed charmed with the original. There may, perhaps, be some choice expression, and some excellence of arrangement, that can not be shown in translation. (No doubt of this.)

After we exhausted the Erse poems, of which Dr. Johnson said nothing, Miss MacLean gave us several tunes on a spinnet, which, though made so long ago as in 1667, was still very well toned. She sung along with it. Dr. Johnson seemed pleased with the music, though he owns he neither likes it, nor has hardly any perception of it."

Dr. Johnson himself says in his own Journal :—

"There has lately been in the Islands one of those illiterate poets, who, hearing the Bible read at church, is said to have turned the sacred history into verse. I heard part of a dialogue composed by him translated by a young lady in Mull, and thought it had more meaning than I expected from a man totally uneducated; but he had some opportunities of knowledge; he lived among a learned people."

Dr. Hector MacLean was the only son of Lachlan MacLean of Grulin. He married Catherine, daughter of Donald MacLean of Coll. He practised for a considerable time in Glasgow; and then went to Mull, where he had the farm of Erray, about a mile and a half from Tobermory. It was here that he took down the songs of John MacLean, and other songs, in a strongly-bound note-book of dimensions twelve inches, by seven and a half inches, by one and a quarter inches.

After the death of the doctor, his daughter, Mary, of whom Boswell and Johnson speaks in the above quotations, kept the book till she handed it to John MacLean, another poet of whom more anon, in the year 1818. John MacLean brought it with him to Canada, and it is now in the possession of Rev. A. MacLean Sinclair. Twenty-two of Iain Mac Ailein's songs appear in the

C

"Glenbard Collection," and other eleven appear in the "Gaelic Bards," both books published by Rev. A. MacLean Sinclair.

DOMHNULL BAN MAC GHILLEAIN, AM MUILE.

This man composed a very good song on Donald MacLean, third of Brolas, who was Lieutenant-colonel under Sir John MacLean, chief of the clan at the battle of Sheriffmuir. The song consists of seventeen verses of eight lines each, and seems to have been composed about 1725. We cannot say who Donald Ban was, or if he composed any other song. He was living during the first quarter of the eighteenth century.

MAIREARAD NIGHEAN LACHUINN.

Mairearad nighean Lachuinn, or Margaret MacLean, composed the most and the best of her songs between 1700 and 1750. She lived all her days in Mull, but it is impossible to fix either the date of her birth or the date of her death. Some have tried to prove that Margaret was a Macdonald, that her mother was a MacLean, and married to a Macdonald. It is unnecessary to investigate the point. A reference to her songs shows that nearly all her songs were composed on MacLeans. We have come across the following :—

1. Do Shir Iain Mac Ghilleain, beginning—
   O, fhuair mi sgeul 's cha'n aicheam e.
   (11 verses of 6 lines.)
2. Duanag do chlann Ghilleain, beginning—
   Cha choma leam fein co dhiu sin.
   (6 verses of 4 lines.)
3. Cumha do Shir Iain Mac Ghilleain, Triath Dhubhairt, a chaochail 's a' bhliadhna, 1716 (Gaoir nam ban Muileach), beginning—
   'S goirt leam gaoir nam ban Muileach.
   (22 verses of 8 lines.)
4. Do dh-Ailein Mac Ghilleain, Fear Bhrolais, beginning—
   Mo cheist an Leathanach modhar.
   (18 verses of 8 lines.)
5. Do Shir Eachuinn Mac Ghilleain a chaochail san Roimh 's a' bhliadhna, 1751, beginning—
   Thir tha 'n Caithir an' Fhreasdail.
   (16 verses of 8 lines.)
6. Do dh-Ailein Mac Ghilleain, Mac Fear Bhrolais, beginning—
   Chunnaic mise thu, Ailein.
   (20 verses of 8 lines.)
7. Cumha do Lachunn Mac Ghilleain, beginning—
   Gur h-e mise th' air mo leonadh.
   (11 verses of 5 lines.)
8. Do Shir Iain Mac Ghilleain, Triath Dhubhairt, beginning—
   Dh-fhalbh mo chadal a' smaoinlinn.
   (9 verses of 4 lines.)

9. Oran do Shir Iain Mac Ghilleain, beginning—
 Ged is stochd mi 'n deigh crionadh.
 (6 verses of 8 lines.)
10. Do dh-Ailein Mac Ghilleain, Fear Bhrolais, beginning—
 Mo run an t-Ailein, marcach, aileil.
 (8 verses of 4 lines.)

REV. JOHN MACLEAN.

Rev. John MacLean, minister of Kilninian and Kilmore in Mull, from 13th September, 1702, till 12th March, 1756, was not only, as testified by the Presbytery of Mull, a man of great zeal for the interest of religion and the dignity of the ministerial character, but the author of several very good poems. He also wrote a complimentary poem to the second edition of Lhuyd's "Archæologia Britannica." I take the following translation of it from Rev. Nigel MacNeill's "Literature of the Highlanders."

Pattison, in his "Gaelic Bards," gives the original Gaelic, and gives a translation which is equal, if not superior, to the one here given.

When the grey Gael—Milesian race from Spain—
To green Ierne had crossed the mighty main,
Great was the fame they carried to our shore,
Of skill in arms, of poetry and lore.
When that good seed had spread out far and near,
The Gaelic then was honoured there and here ;
That musically sweet expressive tongue,
To which our fathers have so fondly clung.

In royal courts, a thousand years and more,
It reigned in honour—spoke from shore to shore ;
Then bard and lyrist, prophet, sage and leech,
Wrote all their records in the Gaelic speech :
Since first Gathelus came from Egypt's strand,
That ancient tongue was written in our land ;
The great divines whose fame is shed abroad,
In Gaelic accents learned to praise their God.

'Twas Gaelic Patrick spoke in Innis-Fayl,
And sainted Calum in Iona's Isle ;
Rich polished France, where highest taste appears,
Received her learning from that Isle of Tears.
Iona, *alma mater* of each tribe and tongue,
Once taught for France and Germany their young !
Well may we now our swelling grief outpour,
That seat in ruin, and our tongue no more !

Great praise and thanks, O noble Lhuyd, be thine,
True learned patriot of the Cambrian line !
Thou hast awaked the Celtic from the tomb,
That our past life her records might illume.
Engraved in every heart, in lettered gold,
Thy name remains: thy silent words unfold
To future ages what our sires had seen,
While others say, "A Gaelic race hath been."

This is the meaning, but it naturally loses a great deal of its force and its terseness in the translation.

AN T-AIREACH MUILEACH.

A Coll correspondent, Mr. J. Johnston, says that An t-Aireach Muileach was Iain mac Eoghain mhic Iain Ruaidh, and that he was nearly related to the Coll family. An t-Aireach was the author of *Crois Dhanachd fir na Drimnin.* Rev. A. MacLean Sinclair states as follows in the Gaelic Bards, page 159 :—

"The Aireach Muileach was a MacLean. He was, as his name imports, a herdsman, and lived in Mull. It is said that he was in the employ of MacLaine of Lochbuie. He had a clear head and a sharp tongue, and was a bitter satirist. A man named Colin Campbell, "An Caimbeulach Dubh," stole some cows from Lochbuie. The Aireach took vengeance upon the thief by composing a song about him. When Mac-Mhaighstir Alastair heard the song. he composed a reply in praise of Campbell. and abused the Aireach in it. This led to a war of words between them. Whilst the Aireach was by no means the equal of Mac-Mhaighstir Alastair in poetic ability, he was more than a match for him as a cutting, stinging satirist." Of the Aireach's song on Campbell, we have seen only two verses.

AN CAIMBEULACH DUBH.

An Caimbeulach Dubh a Ceanntaile
Iar-ogh' mhortair 's ogh a mhearlaich
Am Braid-Albainn fhuair e 'arach—
Siol na ceilge 's mearlach a chruidh.

'S odhar ciar an Caimbeulach Dubh
'S oilteil fiadhaich 'amharc 's a chruth
'S lachdunn liath-ghlas dubh; cha n-fhiach e
'S fear gun mhiadh an Caimbeulach Dubh.

Cuiream tuath e, cuiream deas e,
Cuiream siar e, cuiream sear e,
Cuiream fios gu baird gach fearunn,
Gus an caill e 'chraicionn na shruth.
'S odhar ciar, &c., &c.

IAIN MAC-THEARLAICH-OIG.

John MacLean was the son of Charles MacLean, fifth of Inverscadel, by his second wife. He composed several good songs, his best probably being one about the Act proscribing the Highland dress.

Is ann leam nach 'eil tlachdmhor
An t-Achd a rinn Deorsa,
Thug air n-airm bhuainn 's air n-aodoch
A bha daonnan 'g ar comhdach
'N aite breacan an fheile
As'm bu ghleusda fir oga
Gun ach brigis is casag
Agus bata 'n ar doirnibh.

O marbhaisg ort, a shaoghail
Tha thu caochlaideach, cealgach ;
Bha mi uair nach do shaoil leam
Teachd as aogais a' gharbhlaich.
Mis' a chleachd 'bhi 'n Airdghobhar,
'M bu tric gleadhar bhoc earba
Than an diugh an Sorn odhar
Air todhar a mheanbh-chruidh.

EOGHAN MAC-GHILLEAIN, AM BARRA.

We have come across two of his songs in the "Glenbard
Collection," both of which are of great merit.
1. Oran do Mhac-Neill Bharra.
2. Oran do Thearlach Mor Mac-Ghilleain, Fear na Sgurra.

MALCOLM MACLEAN—CALUM A GHLINNE.

No song in the Gaelic language has attained greater popularity,
or is better known than " Mo chailin donn og." Malcolm
MacLean was a native of Kinlochewe in Ross-shire. He joined
the army, and after getting his discharge and a small pension, he
returned to his native place. Having married a wife whose
virtues were comparable to, if they did not actually surpass, those
of Job, MacLean had every prospect of leading a happy contented
life on his croft at the foot of *Bein Fuathais*. But, alas! in his
soldier days he learned drinking habits, from which he could not
free himself now; nor ever did till his death in 1764.

He had a daughter—an only child—of uncommon beauty.
Owing to the drouthy character of the father, her hand was
unsolicited, and this is the occasion of the song, in which he deals
side blows at hunters for fortunes in wives, and in which he takes
a reasonable share of the blame to himself, for the fact of his
daughter being still unwooed, unsought, and unmarried.

Gu 'm bheil thu gu boidheach
Bainndidh, banail,
Gun chron ort fo' n ghrein,
Gun bheum, gun sgainnir ;
Gur gil' thu fo d' leine
Na eiteag na mara
'S tha coir agam fein
Gun chéile bhi mar-riut.
          Mo chailinn donn òg.

Gur muladach mi
'S mi 'n deigh nach math leam
Na dheanadh dhut stà
Aig cach 'ga mhalairt ;
Bi'dh t-athair an comhnuidh
'G ol le caithream
'Se eolas nan corn
A dh-fhag mi cho falamh.
          Mo chailinn donn òg.

Ge mor le cach
Na tha mi milleadh
Cha tugainn mo bhoid
Nach olainn tuilleadh,
'S e gaol a bhi mor
Tha m' fheoil a' sireadh—
Tha 'n sgeul ud ri aithris
Air Calum a Ghlinne.
Mo chaiłinn donn òg.

I take the following note from "Sar Obair nam Bard," by
John Mackenzie:—

"The virtue of mildness in his wife was often put to the test,
and found to be equal to the glowing representation of the poet.
Malcolm had occasion to go to Dingwall on a summer-day for a
boll of oatmeal, and having experienced the effects of a burning
sun and sultry climate, he very naturally went into a public house
on his way to *refresh* himself. Here he came in contact with a
Badenoch drover, who, like himself, did occasional homage at the
shrine of the red-eyed god. Our "worthy brace of topers" entered
into familiar confab; gill was called after gill, till they got gloriously
happy. Malcolm forgot, or did not choose to remember, his
meal; the drover was equally indifferent about his own proper
calling—and thus they sat and drank, and roared and ranted, until
our poet told his last sixpence on the table. After a pause, and
probably revolving the awkwardness of going home without his
meal, "Well," said Malcolm, "if I had more money I would not
go home for some time yet." "That's easily got," replied his
crony, "I'll buy the grey horse from you." The animal speedily
changed owners, and another and more determined onslaught on
"blue ruin" was the consequence. Our poet did nothing by
halves—he quaffed stoup after stoup, until his pockets were
emptied a second time. "Egad!" exclaimed MacLean, making an
effort to lift his head and open his eyes, "I must go *now.*" "You
must," rejoined his friend, "but I cannot see for the life of me
how you can face your wife." "My wife," exclaimed the bard in
astonishment, "pshaw! man, she's the woman that never said, or
will say, worse to me than, 'Dia leat a Chalum,' that is, 'God
bless you, Malcolm.'" "I'll lay you a bet of the price of the horse
and the meal that her temper is not so good, and that you will get
an entirely different salutation," replied the drover, who had no
great faith in the taciturnity of the female sex. "Done! my
recruit," vociferated the bard, grasping the other by the hand.
Away went Malcolm, and with him the landlord and other two
men, to witness and report what reception our drouthy friend
should meet. He entered his dwelling, and as he approached on
the floor, he staggered and would have fallen in the fire, placed
grateless in the centre of the room, had not his wife flung her
arms affectionately about him, exclaiming, "Dia leat a Chalum."

"Ah!" replied Malcolm, "why speak thus softly to me—I have drunk my money, and brought home no meal." "A heatherbell for that," said his helpmate, "we will soon get more money and meal too." "But," continued the intoxicated poet, "I have also drunk the grey horse." "What signifies that, my love?" rejoined the excellent woman; "You, yourself, are still alive and mine, and never shall we want—never shall I have reason to murmur while my Malcolm is sound and hearty." It was enough: the drover had to count down the money, and in a few hours Mrs. Maclean had the pleasure of hailing her husband's return with the horse and meal."

He composed a song on this incident, of which the Luinneag is :—

Sud mar dh-iomair mi 'n teach odhar
Thug mi thun na féile fodham;
'N uair a shaoil mi 'chur air teadhair
'S ann a gheibhinn drain dheth.

GILLEASBUIG LAIDIR.

Archibald MacLean, known as Gilleasbuig Laidir, was a second cousin of John MacLean, the poet; the father of the former and the grandfather of the latter being brothers. He died in the year 1830. One of his songs appears in "Clarsach na Coille," and other two in the M.S. of John MacLean, now in the possession of Rev. A. MacLean Sinclair.

DOMHNULL BAN NA LIBE.

Donald MacLean, Mull, was a good poet. His best effort is one he composed on Doctor Allan MacLean, Ross, Mull, when he was nearly drowned while on a passage from Mull to Skye. It appears in "The Songster," page 99, and is entitled "Soraidh slan do'n Ailleagan."

Another song of Donald's, "Fonn nam Meirleach" is of repute in Mull. It was composed on certain parties who stole a pet lamb.

AN CUBAIR COLACH.

Alexander MacLean, known as an Cùbair Colach, was a native of Coll. He emigrated to Australia about 1840, where he recently died. He composed many good songs, and we may specially mention

"Air Cuairt do dh-America," 8 verses of 8 lines.
"Oran do bhàta *Struilleag*," 10 verses of 8 lines.

REV. DUNCAN MACLEAN.

Rev. Duncan MacLean was born in July, 1796, in Killin, Perthshire. He studied for the ministry. His first charge was in Benbecula in North Uist, but he afterwards successively ministered in Salen, Mull, in Kilbrandon, and in Glenorchy, where he died in December 1871. He was an able preacher, and his services

were in much request all over the Highlands. He composed
many songs of a devotional character, and hymns. In the year
1868 a small volume of his poems was published in Glasgow,
entitled *Laoidhean agus Dain.* It contains 79 poems, besides 14
translations and 6 elegies. These in poetic merit rank equal to
those of Dugald Buchanan Rannoch, or of John Morison from
Harris.

"A keenly aesthetical spirit pervades all that MacLean has
written; and he has written more than any of the first-class
religious bards. He is exceedingly rich in poetic illustration, and
very profound in thought. He was a man of wide general culture,
and he brought the power and fruits of it with him into the sphere
of Gaelic religious poetry. But though his countrymen highly
appreciated his able administrations in that language in the pulpit,
they do not appear to be ready to understand that they have such
a deep mine of fresh and original thought in his poetry. The
thoughtful reader, however, will at once feel that MacLean is a
man of great culture, and a poet of a high order, in full sympathy
with man and the works of creation. Like Morison of Harris, he
is too profound for the present popular taste."

JOHN MACLEAN, 1787 TO 1848.

John MacLean, known in Scotland as " Bard Tighearna Chola,"
but known in America as "Am Bard MacGhilleain," was a poet of
high merit. He was born in Tiree in 1787. In his school days
he made good progress in reading and writing—showed more
inclination to be in the company of old people, to hear old stories
and old songs, than to join in the sports and amusements of his
fellow scholars. At the age of 16 he was apprenticed to a shoe-
maker, which trade he afterwards practised for a year in Glasgow
and for several years in Tiree. But being of a restless disposition
we find him joining the Militia very much against the wishes and
advice of his friends. Here however he only stayed less than a
year. In 1818 he published a collection of poems, containing 22
poems by himself, and 34 by others. Immediately thereafter he
made up his mind to emigrate to America, a very unwise step for
him personally, for though he was a good poet, he was but a poor
farmer, and hence we find him in very poor circumstances for
many years after his arrival in Pictou and Merigonish. His own
song "A' Choille Ghruamach," bears out the correctness of this
inference.

> Gu bheil mi'm ónrachd 's a' choille ghruamaich
> Mo smaointinn luaineach, cho tog mi fonn ;
> 'Fhuair mi'n taite so'n aghaidh naduir
> Gu'n threig gach tàlanta bha 'nam cheann ;
> Cha dean mi òran a chur air dòigh ann
> 'Nuair ni mi tòiseachadh bidh mi trom
> Chaill mi 'Ghaidhlig seach mar a b' àbhaist dhomh
> 'Nuair a bha mi 's an dúthaich thall.

Cha 'n ioghnadh dhomhsa ged 'tha mi bronach
'Sann tha mo chòmhnuidh air cùl nam beann,
Am meadhon fasaich air amhuinn Bhàrnaidh
Gu'n dad a's fearr na buntàta lom.
Mu'n dean mi aiteach 's mu 'n tog mi bàrr ann
'S a' choille ghabhaidh 'chur as a' bonn
Le neart mo ghàirdein, gu' m bi mi sàraicht'
A's treis air faillinn mu' m fàs a' chlann.

'Si so an duthaich 's a bheil an cruadal
Gun fhios do 'n t-sluagh a tha tigh'nn a nall,
Gur h-olc a fhuaras oirnn luchd a bhuairidh
A rinn le 'n tuairisgeul air toirt ann.
Ma ni iad buannachd cha mhair i buan dhaibh
Cha dean i suas iad 's cha 'n ioghnadh leam,
'S gach mallachd truaghain a bhios 'g an ruagadh
Bho' n chaidh am fuadach a chur fo'n ceann.   -

and so he goes on in the same strain for eighteen verses.

I take a translation of two of the verses of this song from Rev. Nigel MacNeill's "Literature of the Highlanders":—

I stray alone in these woods of shadows,
My thoughts are restless, I feel in pain ;
This place conflicts with the laws of nature,
My strength forsakes me in heart and brain.
I cannot sing the old songs of Albinn,
My bosom saddens to hear their strain ;
My Gaelic dies since I speak no longer
That tongue still cherished beyond the main.

Alas ! small wonder though I sorrow
Behind the hills in this gloomy wood,
In this lone desert by Barney's River,
With bare potatoes alone for food.
Ere cultivation is seen rejoicing
O'er all the land and the trees are cleared,
My strength will fail in an arm exhausted
While yet the children are left unreared.

Evidently the poet was disappointed in America. He depicted it in his imagination before leaving Scotland, as a land flowing with milk and honey. The reality was that he had nothing but bare potatoes, neither cows, nor sheep, and scarcity of clothing. In Scotland he had many friends, and he was fond of society, but in America his nearest neighbour, Kenneth Cameron, was more than two miles distant from him. In 1830 twelve years after he arrived in America, he removed to Glenbard, where he seems to have got on better, as his children were now able to help him. We have reason to believe that his descendants are in affluent and comfortable circumstances.

In 1835 a small but imperfect edition of his poems was published in Glasgow by Maurice Ogle. In 1881 a more complete edition of MacLean's works appeared, edited carefully and very appreciatively by his grandson, Rev. A. MacLean

D

26

Sinclair, a gentleman to whom Gaelic literature owes much. His hymns, 47 in number, appeared in 1880 under the title "Dain Spioradail," edited by the same gentleman.

In 1863 Norman Macdonald, a native of Moidart, and schoolmaster in Antigonish, re-issued MacKenzie's "Sar Obair nam Bard," and I quote the following from Mr. Macdonald's account of John MacLean :—

"The poet had a strong and penetrating intellect, a lofty imagination, and a clear and comprehensive judgment. His poem on America has been greatly admired. The description which he gives of the country, the state of society, the long dreary winters, and the sultry summers is exceedingly graphic and true. His elegy on Mrs. Noble is perhaps unsurpassed by anything of the kind in the Gaelic language. It abounds with similies of the greatest beauty. The bard had a resolute will, a tender and benevolent heart, and a brave and manly spirit. He was always of a quiet and imperturable disposition. His manners were altogether pleasing and winning, his conversational powers were of the highest order : the old and the young listened to him with delight. He was fond of society. Like the generality of bards, he was also fond of a cheerful glass, and sang the praises of "Fear na Toiseachd." His soul was free from malice and resentment ; a satirical venemous poem he never wrote. His whole life was exemplary. He was an affectionate husband, a kind parent, a true friend, and a sincere Christian. He was an enthusiastic Highlander, and never forgot the land of his birth. He was liked and esteemed by all who knew him, and he died without an enemy. The poet was about five feet and nine inches in height, stout, and well-built. He had dark hair and grey eyes, and a broad and massive forehead. His voice was soft and musical, and he was a good singer."

The poet died from the effects of a cold, in the year 1848, survived by his wife, who died on June 5th, 1877, and three sons and two daughters.

Rev. A. MacLean Sinclair recently published a small pamphlet giving a brief genealogical account of the MacLeans of Glenbard, tracing them up to Gilleain the founder and first chief of the Clan MacLean, who lived in Argyllshire about the year 1250. The pamphlet is very interesting, and the information it contains may be authentic.

DOMHNULL CUBAIR.

Donald MacLean, known as Domhnull Cubair, was second son of Allan MacLean, and brother of John MacLean the Poet. He was born in 1770, and died in 1868 in the 98th year of his age. He is said to have composed several short songs.

27

CHARLES MACLEAN.

Charles MacLean was the eldest son of John MacLean the Poet. He was born in Tiree, 24th July, 1813. He died 27th June, 1880. He composed some songs of merit. Two of them are given in "Clarsach na Coille."

LACHLAN MACLEAN, 1799 TO 1845.

Lachlan MacLean was a native of Coll, and latterly was a hosier in Glasgow, where, on that account he was better known as Lachunn na' Mogan. In 1828 he edited a book of hymns by John Morrison from Skye, and he got permission to include in it three of his own hymns. There is also one of his songs in "Clarsach na Coille."

> SEISD—'S iad na Gaidheil fein na diùlaich
> Ho ho, hi ri il ù oh.
> 'S iad na Gaidheil fein na diùlaich.
>
> 'S iad na Gaidheil fein na gaisgich
> 'S fad 's is farsuing a chaidh cliu orr'.
>
> Faigheadh iad cothrom na Feinn
> 'S co air reilean a bheir cuis dhiubh.

But Lachlan MacLean is better known as the author of "Adam and Eve," a curious book, in which he tries to prove that it was Gaelic that Adam and Eve spoke. It was published in 1837. He wrote many other books, and a large number of interesting and scholarly articles in the "Teachdaire Gaidhealach," and in "Cuairtear nan Gleann," under the *nom-de-plume* of "Mac-Talla."

JOHN MACLEAN, SKYE.

John MacLean was a native of Waternish in the Isle of Skye. His father, Norman MacLean married a St. Kilda woman, who was therefore known in the district as Mor Irteach. John himself was a sailor. He died at Liverpool in 1878. Two of his songs appear in "The Songster"—"Thug mi gaol do'n t-seoladair," "A ho ro, mo Mhairi lurach."

The first is supposed to be composed by his sweetheart to himself, in which she gives expression to her fears regarding his constancy to her, while roaming far and wide throughout the world; and the second is supposed to be an answer trying to allay her fears in this direction.

I quote three verses from "Thug mi gaol do'n t-seoladair."

> Gur lionmhor mais' ri aireamh
> Air an armunn dh-fhas gun mheang,
> Gu'n aithnichinn fein air faireadh thu
> 'S tu àrd air bharr nam beann :

28

Bu deas air ùrlar claraidh thu,
'N uair thairneadh tu'n tigh-dhanns —
Troigh chuimir am bròig chluaiseinich
'S gach gruagach ort an geall !

Ach innsidh mise 'n fhirinn duibh —
Mur bheil mo bharail faoin,
Tha gaol nam fear cho caochlaideach
'S e 'seoladh mar a' ghaoth,
Mar dhriuchd air madainn cheitein,
'S mar dhealt air bhàrr an fheòir ;
Le teas na grèine eiridh e
'S cha leir dhuinn e 's na neoil.

'S ma 's ni e nach 'eil ordaichte,
Gu'n comhlaich sinn gu brath,
Mo dhurachd thu bhi fallain
'S mo roghainn ort thar chaich !
Ma bhrist thu 'nis na cumhnantan
'S nach cuimhne leat mar bha
Guidheam rogha ceile dhuit
A's laidhe 's eirigh slàn !

Mr Henry Whyte (Fionn) has given an excellent translation of
this song, which he has included in his " Celtic Garland." I shall
only quote the last verse :—

And if stern fate has ordered so,
That we shall meet no more ;
And if by thee forgotten are
Our vows upon the shore ;
I'll pray that health and happiness
May ever with thee stay—
A charming wife to comfort thee,
And cheer thee on thy way.

REV. ALEX. THOMSON MACLEAN, 1832 TO 1882.

A good account of the life and works of the Rev. Alex. Thomson
MacLean is given in Edward's " Living Poets," from which the
following notes are for the most part taken.

He was born in Glasgow on the 18th June, 1832, and he
died in Baillieston on 6th July, 1882. He was the son of a
warehouseman, a man of intelligence and moral qualities much
beyond those of his class. His mother was a sister of
George Donald, who was author of " Lays of the Covenanters,"
and of the most gifted of the contributions to the " Whistle
Binkie" and " Nursury Songs." His father died while he
was still young, leaving himself and two sisters to the care of
his mother. She removed with them to Pollokshaws. Here
Alexander was put to employment in a public work. But he
attended evening classes, and thus made up for the deficiency of
his school days. We are told that he was in the habit, after his
daily toil, of sitting up late, and that the mental work he thus per-
formed during his early years was immense. Shortly after, he had
the good fortune of getting the favour and help of Lady Maxwell

of Pollok, who provided a school-room for him to undertake the teaching of pupils. By this means he was enabled to attend the University of Glasgow; and in due course he was licensed as a preacher in connection with the United Presbyterian denomination. He was minister of the U.P. church at Baillieston till his death.

Mr. MacLean commenced early to write verses, his first effusions being published in the Glasgow and other newspapers. In 1857 he issued a volume, entitled "Oran and other Poems," which was very favourably reviewed by the press. The principal poem is a lengthy dramatic piece in blank verse, interspersed with several lyrics. The structure of the poem is in keeping with dramatic requirements, the characters of the *dramatis personæ* being consistently sustained, and the subjects managed throughout with remarkable unity and effect. "Oran" contains many passages of lofty poetry expressed in a terse and vigorous style; and numerous gems of thought, descriptive, moral, and philosophical, might be culled from it.

Mr. MacLean's minor poems are characterised by an easy vivacity and vigour of expression, lively fancy, imagination and pathos, and they evince a ready command of the essential constituents of poetical composition. He has, under the various *noms-de-plume* of "Delta," "Christopher South," "Asmodais," published many pieces, all invariably meritorious. In 1883, a memorial volume of him was issued by his son. It contains a biographical sketch, and includes selections from his writings in poetry, prose, and sermons, extending to 320 pages. A series of essays under the name "Noctes Bailliestonianae" are exceedingly racy and interesting.

We are told that Mr. MacLean's pulpit discourses were earnest and effective, the outcome of a robust intellect and a heart animated by deep religious feeling. While zealous in proclaiming the everlasting truths of a pure gospel, he was careful to avoid the hackneyed paths of a cold and formal theology. He poured forth his thoughts in fervid language, untrammelled by pedantic conventionalities, and he enlivened and enforced his utterances by drawing from the rich stores of a highly cultured mind.

WILLIAM MACLEAN OF PLANTATION.

William MacLean of Plantation, father of our treasurer, was not only a poet of a very high order, but a musical composer of some eminence. His two dramas, "Brennus" and "Alcander" are worthy of a place beside those of Shakespeare, which they so much resemble. Meantime, without entering into any critical dissertation of those pieces, I shall content myself by quoting the following notice from the *Glasgow Herald*, 29th Nov., 1892 :—

"DEATH OF MR. WILLIAM MACLEAN OF PLANTATION.—We regret to record the death of this old and much-esteemed citizen,

which took place early yesterday evening at his residence, 188 West Regent Street. Mr. MacLean had been for some time in failing health ; but while his physical strength was decaying, his mental powers remained clear and vigorous to the last, and his end was entirely peaceful. Mr. MacLean was in his 88th year, having been born in Glasgow in March, 1805. He was the eldest son of Mr. William MacLean of Plantation, one of the magistrates of the City, whose estate, situated between Glasgow and Govan, is now almost entirely feued for dwelling-houses and works, while the old mansion-house, one of our ancient landmarks, is at present in course of demolition. For many years he was in partnership with his father and Mr. William Brodie of Endrick Bank, first as manufacturers, and afterwards as cotton spinners, at Eaglesham. He was a Justice of the Peace for the counties of Lanark and Renfrew, and long took great interest in the business of the Courts, where he often presided. He was long a director of the Royal Infirmary and other institutions. Work of this kind was congenial to his nature, which found exercise in various ways, such as relieving poverty and distress, and seeking situations for the unemployed. In early days, prior to the passing of the Reform Bill, Mr. MacLean was an ardent supporter of the Liberal cause : but he was opposed to the dismemberment of the empire, and at last election showed his adhesion to Unionist principles by voting for Mr. Baird in the Central Division, and for Mr. Spens at Govan. Though never taking office except as a manager, he was an influential member of the United Presbyterian Church, and warmly attached to evangelical doctrines. He was distinguished for his musical and poetic tastes. Among his publications in early life were "Christian Poems," and, later on, two dramatic pieces, "Brennus" and "Alcander," which, with his other writings, were much appreciated by his friends. He composed a very large number of sacred melodies, including several well-known psalm and hymn tunes. One of his latest productions was a loyal ode, both words and music of which were his own, written on the occasion of Her Majesty's visit to the International Exhibition in Glasgow in 1888, a copy of which was graciously accepted by the Queen. Notably polite and courteous, and of much amiability of temper, Mr. MacLean was punctilious in his attention to small matters At the same time, in the trying experiences of life, he showed strength of character and sense of duty. Wise in counsel, shrewd and sagacious as well as sympathetic, many sought his advice and assistance in seasons of difficulty, ever assured of his guidance and help. Mr. MacLean married a daughter of the Rev. Robert Muter, D.D., minister of the then Duke Street Secession Church. His wife predeceased him fourteen years ago, but he is survived by a family of eight—three sons and five daughters."

31

LOYAL ODE.

(On occasion of Her Majesty's visit to Glasgow, 18th August, 1888.)

Long may Victoria reign
O'er Britain's vast domain
    And deck the throne !
The world has never seen
So true and loved a Queen
As thou hast ever been,
    Empress alone !

Great wise Victoria,
Thy sovereign power and law
    Adorn the world,
Thy love redeems the slave,
Thy troops are leal and brave,
Thy sailors ride the wave
    With flag unfurled !

Science and Art now fill
The wide earth with their skill,
    And own thy sway !
Under thy favoured Crown,
Blessings from Heaven flow down
On forest, field, and town,
    Both night and day !

Mr. William MacI can also presented to the Mitchell Library a collection of sacred melodies, accompanied by the following letter :—

"Glasgow, 5th January, 1885,
188 West Regent Street.

My Dear Sir,

According to promise I now present to the Mitchell Library the MS. volume of sacred melodies (close upon 3000) composed by me, and I do so in the hope that it may be of some service to students of music. In the composition of this work, it has been my aim to form musical cadences adapted to the many varied emotional utterances of our national sacred poetry, and, as far as I am aware, without having copied the work of any other composer.

I am,

William Wilson, Esq.,   My dear sir,
    Chairman of the   Very truly yours,
        Mitchell Library Committee.   . WILLIAM MACLEAN.

There are three supplements to this volume, one in 1885, a second in 1886, and a third in 1887.

I take the following account of the first volume all in MS. from the *North British Daily Mail*, Wednesday, 7th January, 1885 :-

"A REMARKABLE MUSIC BOOK.

"There has just been presented to the Mitchell Library a volume of music which in some respects is unequalled, and which, we believe, will be peculiarly interesting to all lovers of sacred

song. It is entitled 'Sacred Melodies,' and contains the unparalleled number of 2881 tunes and chants, the whole being composed by our esteemed townsman, William MacLean, Esq., of Plantation, J.P. That such an enormous number of original tunes should be composed by one individual seems almost incredible; but this has been accomplished by Mr. MacLean in a manner which will, we think, free him from any charge of plagiarism. The tunes are divided into four great classes—iambic, trochaic, dactylic, and anapæstic; and these, again, are subdivided into numerous metres, suitable for the psalms and nearly all the hymns at present used in our churches. We understand that Mr. MacLean has been engaged composing these tunes during the last thirty years, never slavishly, but writing only when the ideas were suggested to his mind. About that time he published a selection of two hundred tunes, which were all very effectively harmonised by several local musicians. This volume, a copy of which we have in our possession, has been out of print for some time. The first quality in a psalm or hymn tune, it will be readily admitted, is melody; for so long as the air is sung by the majority of people in our congregations, those tunes will always be the most popular which have an attractive melody in the air. Hence the reason that such tunes as 'New Henley,' 'Derby,' 'St. Marnock's,' 'Orlington,' and many others were so popular in bygone days; and those who remember with what power and effect these tunes were sung long ago, will think the singing of our congregations nowadays very tame indeed. The modern tunes composed by our great musicians, and which fill the pages of our new hymn-books, are, generally speaking, singularly destitute of melody, and depend for their effects altogether upon their harmonies. It would seem as if their authors vied with each other in producing novel and striking chords at the expense of the melody, which, as a rule, receives but scanty consideration. In the book now before us, the tunes are not harmonised, but consist of simple melodies only; and we soon find that Mr. MacLean is the happy possessor of a talent for melody which very few can lay claim to. We can scarcely open a page but we find contrast, reply, imitation, or sequence, and always of the most natural and pleasing description. The peculiar metre tunes are specially good. We cannot here particularise the excellent specimens that occur to us, they are so numerous; but would remark that among the 6,5s., the 7,6s., the 4,7s., and the 6.6.4.6.6.6.4s., will be found many tunes well worthy of attention. We congratulate Mr. MacLean on having produced such a book, and trust it may prove useful to editors and others interested in the improvement of psalmody. The volume is in manuscript, and has been executed in a very tasteful manner by Mr. Robert D. Jamieson, leader of psalmody in Free St. Stephen's Church."

33

J. C. MACLEAN.

I have come across the following book, but I have been unable to obtain any information about the author.

LEISURE LYRICS,
BEING
GAIETIES AND GRAVITIES OF VERSE,
BY J. C. MACLEAN,
GLASGOW, 1843.

There are eighty-three pages, and some of the songs are very good. I quote from "Never Despair":—

Can sighing aught improve ye,
Or shedding tears avail;
Will fortune aught more love ye,
For looking sad and pale?

Come throw away this moping
And brooding all alone,
Betake yourself to hoping,
And half your grief is gone.

Dame fortune loves the smiling,
And those who slight her frown,
And laughing, on go toiling.
She raises from the ground.

Nil Desperandum aye then,
Laugh common cares away,
Ne'er heed what cynics say then,
In sad and solemn way.

But wipe away your tear drops,
Nor let your wrinkles grow;
Earth still has love and dear hopes,
If gaily on we go.

The same ideas are expressed in another song—

The cares and moils of wordly strife
If met good-humoured smiling,
May smooth the roughness of our life,
And guide our markest toiling.

JOHN MACLEAN (CLAN BARD).

John MacLean, Bard to the Clan MacLean Association, was born in Tiree, in 1827, and he has been living there ever since.

Two of his pieces are in the "Coisir Chiuil"—the St. Columba collection of Gaelic songs, namely:—"A Chailinn mhaiseach dhonn," and "Hi oro 's na horo eile." "Breacan Mairi Uisdean" is perhaps one of his best known songs.

On communicating with him *re* this paper, he sent the following song:—

34

ORAN DO CHLOINN GHILLEAIN.

LE IAIN MAC GHILLEAIN, TIREADH, BARD A' CHOMUINN.
AIR FONN:—*Mo run geal dileas.*

SEISD—Oh, 's ann an Glaschu nan stlobull àrda
Tha clann nan Gàidheal a nis gu léir,
A' cumail cumhn' air na gaisgich chliuiteach,
A ghleidh an diuthaich d'an sliochd na'n déigh.

Fhuair mi litir 'o shàr dhuin'-uasal
A rinn mo ghluasad o'n àm so 'n dé
'S na 'm biodh e 'làthair 's mi chuireadh fàilt' air
Gu cridheil càirdeil air sgàth a sgeul'.

Mu chlann Ghilleain nan lann 's nan lùth chleas.
Bu deas a dhùisgeadh gu dol air ghleus
Bhi cruinn an Glaschu fo'n ceann-àrmailt'
Na treun laoich chalma bu gharbh am beum.

'S e fir nan clogaid nan sgiath 's nan lùireach,
'S nan lanna rùisgte 'bu mhath gu streup,
An iolair' gharg, fuilteach, fraochar, feargach,
Nam bratach gharbh air bhàrr chrannaibh réidh.

Air Ionarchéitean bha iomadh dearbhadh,
Air fuil bhras mheaumnach nam fear nach géill,
'N uair 'theich an Reiseimaid each, le'n ceannard,
Có sheas 'san àm sin ach clann nan treun!

Ar rìgh 's ar dùthaich, 'se chosg gu daor dhuinn,
An àireamh laoch sin a thuit 'san streup,
An là ud "Gaoir nam ban Muileach," chualas,
'S bheir sinne luaidh orra 'n diugh na'n déigh.

Thug eachdraidh seanachas mar chinneadh ainmeil
Gur tric a dh'fhalbh iad le coin air éill,
Fo chrios-bhall airgid 'us a lharc fhùdair,
Air feadh nan stiichd-bheann le gunn' air ghleus.

'S air lochan glan 'o shruth-bras nam fuar-bheann,
An eal' air uachdar, 'us breac a leum,
Le slait ag iasgach nam bradan tarra-gheal,
'S a siubhal garbhlaich gu sealg an fhéidh.

Le brogan fraochain 'us osain bhalla-bhreac,
Sgian dubh 's i lanna ghorm fo ghartan réidh,
Sporan garbh bhruic mu ghlùnnan ghaisgeach,
Air féileadh snasmhor d' am breacan féin.

Le cóta riomhach 'us breacan guaille,
'Sgach ni bu dual dhaibh bhi air an réir,
Boineid ghorm agus ite 'n fhir-coin.
'S le dùth'chas sloda mar urram beus.

ANDREW MACLEAN.

Andrew MacLean was born in the village of Renton,
Dumbartonshire, in the year 1848. After leaving the parish
school of Alexandria, to which his parents had removed while he

was still an infant, he was apprenticed to the joiner trade in the print works of that place. At the age of fourteen, however, we find him working his passage across the Atlantic—joining the United States navy, wherein he served till the end of the war. He then joined a commercial college in the city of Brooklyn, so as to fit him for the work of a newspaper reporter. A writer, in 1883, says of him :—

"For the past twelve years Mr. MacLean has been steadily employed in Brooklyn journalism, and for eight years he has been managing editor of the *Eagle*. He is an eloquent and effective public speaker, and the skill and ability he has displayed in conducting an influential 'daily' are generally admitted. Engaged as he is, he has but few leisure hours to devote to poetry; and yet such is the energy of the man that he has actually written much—no small portion of which bears the stamp of poetical genius. His poetry shows spontaneity, freshness, and truth; the descriptive and narrative in particular being full of subtle touches and bits of life—like portraiture, and always appreciative and pathetic."

FROM THE SOURCE TO THE SEA.

A clear little rill ran with musical measure
Through scenes that were sylvan and sacred to pleasure,
From under an ash tree, by pine trees surrounded,
Its young current broke free and babbled and bounded ;
Then out of the shade, and away from the dun
Like a boy to his games, sped to play with the sun.

To a landscape of sand, 'twixt the croft and the sea,
As arid and tanned as the heart of Chaldee,
Came the brook rippling cheery—a current of light,
A joy to the weary, a gem to the sight ;
But alas for the glory of woodland and mead,
In the sand died the glitter, the music, the speed.

Oh ! freshness of childhood ! oh, gladness of prime,
Oh, home in the wildwood ! oh, drawing of time,
From thee do we haste to the levels of life,
To the passionate waste, to the toil and the strife,
Where our courage succumbs and our happy hope flee,
Ere we reach the dim shore of the mist-shrouded sea.

DUNCAN MACLEAN.

Duncan MacLean is one of our most prolific Scotch poets. He was born at Dunoon, in 1857, and when he left school he was employed in the Parochial Board office—first as clerk, and afterwards as Assistant Inspector of Poor—altogether four years. We find him in the Glasgow Post Office for a couple of years, then as clerk in the office of the Globe Parcel Express Company, and now in Manchester, where he is manager to that company.

In 1880 Mr. MacLean issued a volume of poems, entitled "Hamely Rhymes." Since then he has been a frequent contributor to the poetical columns of several newspapers. "He

is a pure, pleasing, and graceful writer, and all his thoughts are instinct with a warm and elevating enthusiasm. His Doric is terse, felicitous, and expressive, and while his poems on the beauties of nature are in a fine appreciative vein, and full of graphic and picturesque description, we find present the natural flow of spontaneity and the rhythm full of melody."

I take the following extracts from some correspondence I had with Mr. Duncan MacLean :—

"Being a native of Dunoon, my surroundings were literally permeated with poetry, and though now over ten years in Manchester, my heart still goes back to the dearest spot on earth —home, sweet home.

I am a MacLean out and out. My father was a native of Cowal, and my mother, before her marriage, was a MacLean. A number of years ago I was a very frequent contributor to the *Oban Times, Highland Magazine*, &c. . . . Of late years my business responsibilities are greater, and now I cannot devote the same time to poetical efforts as formerly. . . . I have a large and miscellaneous collection of poems, &c., in printed form and in MS., which, if you care to wade through, I shall gladly make up in a parcel and send them on, in the hope that the perusal would repay the trouble. Apart altogether from the honour of being incorporated with the 'MacLean Bards,' I should in all probability benefit from the estimate you placed on my productions, for though personally unknown to me, and *vice versa*, still I know you by repute."

The letter accompanying the parcel of his MS. poems, &c., contained :—There are two poems in particular to which I would draw your attention and solicit your opinion. They are both in MS., and are entitled "The Dream," a sort of allegorial poem ; and "The Balgie," a long screed full of ruminations, in blank verse.

I published a book of poems, extending to 160 pages, about eleven years ago, when the blossom was in the bud, but as I attach no importance to that premature production, I do not send it you, simply mention it by the way.

I used to advocate the Crofters' question very strongly, and though my enthusiasm has not waned, I find my time is fully occupied by things, though probably not so congenial, still of more practical importance to me.

My brother's poetical flights of fancy are not quite so prolific as mine. He was apprenticed to the engineering trade in Glasgow, but unfortunately never did any good at it, and after drifting about for a number of years, I took him under my wing, and here he has been for the last two years, clerking in the Globe. He writes very good poetry. . . . He is twenty-seven years of age, and I am thirty-five.

37

The following may be taken as a specimen of the songs of Duncan MacLean :—

THE CROFTERS.

From the dark and rugged Highlands there has risen up a cry
That should stir the hearts of millions, and bedim each honest eye;
That should rouse the God of Justice, and make Error shrink with fear;
That should stifle slaves of Mammon in their wild, head-long career.
Oh ! the Highlands, grand and lovely, with their mem'ries dear and strong—
With their proud historic heroes, handed down in deathless song—
Are harassed and landlord-ridden, till the hearts of peaceful men
Have been roused to sudden action, by each beauteous strath and glen.

'Tis a wild and startling story—'Tis a blot on Britain's page
That eclipses in its madness every quibble of our age :
Hard to think that honest peasants, who have tilled and owned their land,
Should be hounded off by tyrants; forced to seek a foreign strand—
Forced to leave each glen and valley that was dear to them as life—
Forced to leave their lowly shielings—oh ! 'twas sharp as edged knife !
Where the pibroch, loud and thrilling, woke the echoes of each glen.
There is nothing now but wailing, caused by cruel, heartless men.

Oh, ye Highlanders, be fearless ! ye but battle for your own—
Ye but strive to sweep proud landlords from a self-erected throne;
For these mountains, heather crested, that tower up to meet the sky
Were not made for cruel sportsmen by the God who reigns on high.
All the world was formed in beauty, all the loveliness and worth
Were as free to honest peasants as the peer of noble birth.
For the Lord of earth and heaven made the world for all mankind :
'Tis the selfish slaves of Mammon who to rob us are inclined.

Oh, ye Highlanders, be constant ! for the day is drawing nigh
When all misery and oppression shall be driven from your sky,
And the glens that owned their thousands when our fathers were in life
Shall once more spring into vigour when God endeth all our strife.
Then your sheep shall bleat their music by the sweet and tinkling rills,
While your cows shall browse in plenty on the daisy-speckled hills;
And prosperity shall flourish in the midst of every glen
When the chain of landlord terror's burst asunder by our men.

Oh ! ye Highlanders of Lewis, and ye sturdy men of Skye,
Shout together in your hundreds till the heavens shall reply—
Till the mists of Wrong and Darkness shall fly to their dismal tomb.
And the Highlands once more cheerful, shall be free from care and gloom.
By each lovely glen and valley, by each rugged mountain side,
Where the purple heather bloometh and the thistle grows with pride—
Where the streams in beauty floweth, where the cataracts so grand,
Flash their treasures in the sunlight : shout, my brethren, for your land !

Oh ! ye Highlanders of Dornoch, and ye sons of dark Portree,
All the young shoots of your kindred have been banished o'er the sea .
And your stalwart sons have fallen in the thickest of the fight,
While the foemen fled in terror 'fore the grandeur of their might.
Yet base landlords call thee cravens, and would sweep ye from the earth,
And then confiscate the hamlets that gave noble heroes birth.
Then rouse ye, oh my brethren ! from each clachan, hill, and glen,
Till the genial glow of Freedom shall light up your souls again.

38

Oh ! ye Highlanders of Morven, and ye sons of Appin, too,
Be united in your efforts to destroy this alien crew;
Ye have borne with matchless patience all their infamy and scorn—
Ye have seen your grey-haired fathers swept from crofts where they were born—
Ye have seen your sons and daughters breadless, houseless, starved and cold,
By these monsters men call human, in their wretched race for gold.
Then rouse my struggling brethren ! by the God we all adore
Till the lands your fathers cherished shall return to you once more.

Oh ! ye brave Lochaber heroes, and ye martyrs of Glencoe,
Be a phalanx, strong and powerful, to oppose your common foe;
Ye have been oppressed for ages, and no murmur passed your lips,
While your dear ones have been banished 'cross the ocean in great ships.
Ye have seen your aged mothers die upon the bleak hillside—
Ye have seen your wives and sisters shedding tears they could not hide:
Ye have slept upon the moorland, while the stars shone overhead,
Cause these monsters of oppression left ye neither home or bed.

Oh ! ye Highlanders of Islay and wild Jura, every clan,
Sound your slogan in the valleys as ye rush forth in the van;
With the strength of mighty mountains your ancestors long ago
Made the foeman flee at Alma, as the sunbeams melt the snow.
Then rouse ye, oh my brethern ; there is work for all to do,
Ere the Highlands—land of heroes !--shall get meted out their due :
'Tis a black and dismal story, but the Right is all your own,
And these greedy, grasping landlords soon shall topple from their throne.

Oh ! ye sprouts of famed Culloden, and ye chieftains of Glenroy,
In your lovely straths and valleys there remaineth little joy,
For the god of fleeting riches has usurped the God of Right.
And the crofts that sweetly flourished have now vanished 'neath man's might.
Ye could tell a tale of sorrow that would make the angels weep ;
Ye could point to cairns where martyrs in the cause of Freedom sleep;
Ye could tell of mighty heroes who at Balaclava fell.
'Mid the crack of hissing bullet and the piproch's magic yell.

Oh, ye Highlanders, be steady ! for the cause ye fight is good—
'Tis a death blow at oppression, that shall bring your children food—
'Tis a cry of human anguish that might melt a heart of stone—
'Tis a sermon pure and holy that appeals to hut and throne—
'Tis a wail of down-trod manhood, asking for their rights again ;
And the God of Love and Wisdom has not heard their cry in vain,
For a mighty wave of feeling has now swept from shore to shore,
And the crofters, proud and loyal, shall get back their land once more.

Oh, ye Highlanders, have courage ! rouse to action one and all !
Tyrants cannot reign for ever, might 'fore right must quickly fall ;
And the land ye long have cherished with devotion past all praise,
Shall once more resound with laughter 'neath the light of brighter days :
For the world has heard your message—it has thrilled them to the core,
It has startled human nature as nought else has done before;
And the dawn of Right is breaking o'er each lovely Highland glen,
That is bringing Peace and Freedom to our noble Highland men.

HUGH ARCHIBALD MACLEAN.

Hugh Archibald MacLean, brother to Duncan, has also written a considerable quantity of good poetry. He was apprenticed to

the engineering trade. On account of bad times, and very probably due to other causes also, Hugh seems to have had a rather chequered career as an engineer; which trade he has finally left, and he is now along with his brother in the employment of the Globe Parcel Express Company in Manchester. "He loves to praise the beauties of his native Caledonia. He possesses a happy lyrical style that is admirable both for natural flow and poetic thought, and that readily lends itself to musical setting. In many of his poems we find patriotism, independence, and an ardent love of the 'Auld Hoos at Hame,' exemplified in a marked degree."

NEIL MACLAINE.

Neil MacLaine, a native of Tiree, and now living in Glasgow, composed several songs. "Caisteal Dhomhnuill's 'a Mhointich na shineadh" is one well known in Tiree. In connection with the first gathering of the Clan MacLean Association in Glasgow, on 28th October, he composed the following :—

Air—" Manitoba."

Fonn.—Tha tional tha tional an drasd aig gach cinneadh,
Tha tional tha tional aig gach cinneadh an drasd,
Cloinn Ghilleain a tional air an ochda la fichead,
'Bidh aighear 'us iomairt aig gillean mo ghraidh.

Gur mis tha gu h-eibhinn 'sa' mhaduinn 's mi g-eirigh
O'n chula mi sgeul a thog gleus air mo chail,
Mu chinne nam feile bhi coinneachadh ri cheile,
Cloinn Ghilleain nan genr-lann nach geileadh do namh.

Le Ceann-Cinnidh tha macant d'an dual a bhi beachdail,
O Dhubhairt a Chaisteal be sud cleacdhadh nan sar ;
Gu 'n seasadh iad dileas an onair na Rioghachd,
Tha eachdruidh ag innseadh mu'n gniomhan 'sna blair.

'Nuair sgaoileas a bhratach bidh tional air gaisgich,
O'n iar 'us o'n ear thig iad air as gach cearn,
Le fior fhuil gun truailleadh nan cuislean a bualadh,
Bhi dileas bu dual doibh gu buaidh no gu bas.

Bha na Leathanaich ainmeil 's gach cearn as do dh' fhalbh iad
Mar leomhan 'us colg air bu dombh dho! nan dail,
Cha bu spiochdairean cruaidh iad n'an nadur-bha 'n uaisle
Gun tric rinn iad fuasgladh air truaighan na'n cas.

Nad shuaicheantas fiochal tha bratan an fhior-uisg,
'San iolair tha riogail a direadh an aird,
Roin a bhian riamhaich 'us long nan crann direach,
Lamh dhearg le cros sinnt Caisteal didean 'us mam.

Sud a choill bha gun chrionach 'san stochd o'n do chinn thu,
'S iomia meanglan priseil a dhirich an aird,
Eadar Carsaig, 's Lochbuidhe 's Torloisgt ann am Muile,
Aird-ghobhar nan curaidh 'us Dubhairt nan sar.

Bha teaghlach nan Colach Ian meas agus onair,
Gum b'fhoigeantach fearail am Breachdlachadh dh'fhas
Cha bu shugradh am fearg nuair a dhuisgeadh an colg
Bhiodh e n' cunntas na marbh ge b'e theargadh tigh'nn dan.

'Sioma ceatharnach, ainmeil do theaghlach nan Druimnin
Nuair thoisicheadh iorgail le'm b'ionmhuinn am blar,
Siad le'n cinneadh air thoiseach aig latha Chuil-fhodair,
'Mar mhiol choin air lomhain air son a bhi sas.

An t-oighr' thig ad dheigh-sa air Cinne-na-feile,
Na di'-chuimhnicheadh e beusan nan treun laoch o'n d'fhas,
Biedh e iochdar ri truaghain 's ri dilleachdain shuarach,
'Sa 'Ghaidhlig bidh uailse air luaidh leis na Baird.

MAGGIE MACLEAN.

Maggie MacLean is a young poetess from Skye, of great promise.
Two of her productions appear in Parlane's "National Choir," set to
music by Alan Reid. I got the two following pieces from herself
in manuscript form :—

THE SONG OF THULE.

I.

Many a time i' the hall o' our sires,
While night nestles low i' the breast o' the vale,
Shall we children o' Leodach rekindle the fires
That ever abide i' the heart o' the Gael.
Through the balmy shadows o' mist that loom
O'er the brown moors, merry and gay,
We shall ride by the scented broom,
But never again wi' Thule.

II.

When the daisies like snow-flakes wave
O'er the emerald robe o' summer,
Our voices shall cease to be grave
To welcome the glad new-comer,
An' the rocks our far-reaching halloo
Shall shout till the tall pines sway,
An' we shall trample the beaded dew,
But never again wi' Thule.

III.

O'er many joys yet shall we smile,
Many sorrows shall win our tears,
An' doubts shall our faiths beguile
To enter the vaults o' fears.
We shall break the peaceful repose
O' seas, lashing blue to gray,
Wi' the oars and vengeance o' foes
But never again wi' Thule.

IV.

When the tempests o' life are over,
An' vices from virtues we sever,
Over our spirits shall hover
The angels o' peace forever.

41

We shall see the pure souls gleaming
I' the light o' God's deathless day,
An' real we shall be not seeming,
Ever again wi' Thulé.

The following lines are from a piece called "Cuthullin."
Cuthullin is the name of an imaginary hero of the past, and the
moor is called after him.

Down in the vale below, in many a humble home,
By the lurid fires of peat, when the moaning spirits of woe,
On the sable wings of night, in the wreaths of darkness come
To dwell in the wild keep, in voices measured and low,
Imbued with the troubled souls which over the marshes roam,
      The old men tell of Cuthullin.

Oft have I dreamed of him, and the eyes of the sages seen
Flash forth the fire of their hearts which cherish those legends well,
But I speak of traditions and days which many years past have been,
The sages are passed away ; there is no one left to tell
Of the spirit of my hero, but the ivy is ever green
      Where it weeps on Cuthullin.

It waters the leaves with its tears ; I have seen in the light of the moon
Shining as silver those tears in the emerald hollows of leaves,
And I think when I hear the waves on the strand of my dear home croon,
That I hear the cry of the soul, its far-reaching cry when it gives
All that it loves to death, all that cries loud " Too soon,"
      Death comes for our Cuthullin.

Science, learnèd and wise, unravels a wondrous store
Of tales concerning the mystical workings of earth and of stars,
Which upheave the faith of my fathers, till doubts that never before
Came nigh the trust of my childhood, have left their obstinate scars
On a sensitive heart already bearing a burden too sore,
      In the loss of its idol Cuthullin.

But wherefore my fretting and weeping ? Will my blustering turn aside
The sorrow that fate has decreed must come to one and to all ?
The gentle voices of Heaven my troubled questionings chide,
Asking, why not my blessings as well as my crosses recall ?
I hear a feeling within me say nothing is ever denied
      The undaunted trust of Cuthullin.

So I turn again to the fountain whence the lips of my childhood drew
The balm of the waters of peace at a truly divine behest.
Already upon the fires of my unbelief the dew
Of its cooling spray is falling, with murmurs lulling to rest
The flames that so hotly smother my happiness when untrue
      To the tender God of Cuthullin.

It behoves me to prove the strength that comes from this joyous trust
In a merciful God, by facing the forces of evil unmoved.
We are prone to suffer the powers most needed by man to rust,
While those which upheave his peace, and should be the least beloved,
We drag in eagerness forth, thus levelling down to the dust
      The teachings of pure Cuthullin.

42

I have searched all the hearts of men, I have searched all the annals of time,
With glances far-reaching and keen, full swift to detect a flaw,
Yet never found purer record ; never impulse so sublime ;
Never actions so guided by a just and generous law ;
Never a mind that sought such lofty summits to climb
   As the great mind of Cuthullin.

Whence came this greatness that speaks to-day to our highest needs,
Intensely as when in the prime of his useful life he spurred
Less by the flow of words than the subtler speech of deeds,
Each comrade and maid of his time to follow a path unblurred ?
Flowers that wither never, ever up-spring from the seeds
   So nobly sown by Cuthullin.

It sprang from the well within, from the promptings of currents divine,
He listened to that still voice which we pause never to hear,
For the great world's feverish aims their short-lived glamours entwine
Around us closely, and smother the prophetic calm of the seer.
In secret we feel through it all ineffaceable cravings pine
   For the even peace of Cuthullin.

Therefore it must needs be that his is the talisman true,
Since never another that gives such perennial solace I find.
Never another from which diviner results accrue,
The badge of its heavenly birth is the record he left behind.
I shall this talisman hold until to another is due
   Life nobler than that of Cuthullin.

Maids of the vales of the Norland ! Sons of the Isles of the free !
Be stirred by the passionate throbbings hopes born of Cuthullin inspire,
His influence pure, in his death, thus strongly hurls forth from me
Words which are teaming and quivering in a furnace of Celtic fire.
His was the land of the Norland ; sons of the Norland should be
   Worthy the gift of Cuthullin !
    etc., etc.

MARY MACLEAN FRANKLIN.

Mary MacLean is the second daughter of Gillespie, son of John
MacLean the Poet. Ten of her songs are given as a kind of
appendix to the genealogical account already referred to. They
are mostly elegies and rhyming hymns. They are simple and
affectionate in tone, and they show a fervent patriotic spirit.

   I once lived in Scotland, the land of the free,
   The land of all others that's dearest to me ;
   But fortune was fickle and did me repel,
   And sent me away from the land loved so well.

   And when in this world all my labours are o'er,
   Pray, carry me back to the dear Scottish shore,
   And lay me to rest in some one of her dells,
   And over my grave plant her bonnie blue bells.

POINTS TO BE CLEARED UP IN THE HISTORY OF THE MACLEANS.*

BY REV. A. MACLEAN SINCLAIR.

I REJOICE that the MacLeans have wakened up to a sense of their duty towards their ancestors, their present chief and chieftains, and one another. They have slumbered a long time, ever since the dark day of Culloden to the present year. I am glad to find that the first object of their Association is "the reviving, fostering, and promoting of clan interests and sentiments, by collecting and preserving records and traditions in any way relating to the Clan." This is a highly praiseworthy object, and one that should be kept in view steadily. The MacLeans have a history, and a history of which they have no reason to be ashamed. By all means, then, let every obtainable fact connected with that history be procured.

Although I am not a MacLean, I have given a fair share, indeed, a very large share, of attention to the history of the MacLeans. It was drilled into my head, and away down into my heart, in my younger days by an intelligent and affectionate mother, who was proud of her clan, and, I rejoice to say, intensely clannish. The man who is not clannish may have a good enough head, a head fitting him for engaging in the work of tracing himself back to monkeys and polliwigs; but I suspect that there must be something wrong with his heart.

In this paper I purpose to deal with some obscure and difficult points in the history of the MacLeans; and also to point out a few mistakes in our published histories.

THE THIRD CHIEF.

According to the valuable MS. of 1467, John Dubh, the fourth chief, was the son of Malcolm, son of Marliosa, son of Gilleain. According to Skene's "History of the Highlanders," page 206, Gillemorr Macilean signed the Ragman Roll in 1296. John Dubh is designated in one place as John Mac Molmari. But Molmari, Maol-Moire, and Gillemorr, Gille-Moire, are the same name.

Skene does not state in what document John Dubh is designated as Maol-Moire. If, however, he is actually designated as such in an official document, I think we must come to the conclusion that the writer of the MS. of 1467 committed a mistake in calling the third chief of the MacLeans, Malcolm. We may regard it as certain that the same man was never called by the two names, Maol Calum or Malcolm, and Maol Moire. The indications in the present state of our knowledge are that the name of the third chief

* Read before the Association on 9th March, 1893

of the MacLeans was Maol-Moire or Gille-Moire, both of which names mean the same thing, Servant of Mary.

In his excellent history of the Clan MacLean, Prof. MacLean advances the theory that Hector Odhar, the ninth chief, was succeeded by his natural son, Lachlan, that Lachlan was killed at the battle of Flodden in 1513, and that he was succeeded by his son, Lachlan Cattanach. In support of his theory, he advances the following arguments :—"Tytler calls the chief who fell at Flodden Lachlan, not Hector. If the chief who fell at Flodden was Hector Odhar, then there were only three chiefs from 1411 to 1513; but it is scarcely possible to believe that there were only three chiefs during that time. It is more than probable that Hector Odhar did not live as late as the year 1500. As Lachlan, the successor of Hector Odhar, was born out of wedlock, it is probable that the family historians suppressed his name to please his immediate successors. Lachlan Cattanach was called by that name, not from having been brought up among the Clan-Chattan, but from his being a hairy, rough, or shaggy man."

I have no faith at all in Prof. MacLean's theory. I believe that Hector Odhar fell at Flodden, and that Lachlan Cattanach, his natural son, succeeded him in the chiefship.

Tytler's statement, that the chief who fell at Flodden was Lachlan, proves nothing. There is no authority given for that statement. I presume that Tytler spoke of the chief who was killed as Lachlan, simply because Lachlan was the legal owner of Duart at the time.

It is quite possible that there were only three chiefs from 1411 to 1513. The MacDonalds were as fond of fighting as the MacLeans, and just as apt to get killed, yet there were only three MacDonald chiefs from 1303 to 1423—Angus Og of Islay; John, first Lord of the Isles; and Donald, second Lord of the Isles, or Donald of Harlaw.

There is not the slightest ground for thinking it more than probable that Lachlan Odhar had died before 1500, or even 1513. Lachlan Lubanach was married in 1365. His son, Hector Rufus Bellorum, Eachunn Ruadh nan Cath, was born probably between 1366 and 1370. Hector's son, Lachlan Bronnach, was born probably about 1391. Lachlan Bronnach would thus be about twenty years of age in 1411. There is no ground whatever for supposing that he was older. According to the author of the Ardgour MS. he was only a young man in 1411. The words of that valuable MS. are these :—"It is likely that he was but a young man when his father went to the battle of Harlaw, and that during his confinement in Mar's house he made up his acquaintance with the daughter, whom he afterwards married; and that

upon her death, he took MacLeod of Harris's daughter for his second wife." *Page 21.* To me, it is not only likely, but certain, that Lachlan Bronnach was a young man in 1411, and that the daughter of Alexander Stewart, Earl of Mar, was his first wife. He was living in 1463. His son and successor, Lachlan Og, may have been born as early as 1415. Lachlan Og had two children, Hector Odhar his heir, and Finvola. Finvola was married in 1462. She was probably, at that time, twenty years of age. The date of her birth, then, would be about the year 1442. Whether she was older or younger than her brother, we do not know. We cannot, however, be far astray in assuming that her brother, Hector Odhar, was born between 1440 and 1450. He would thus be between sixty-three and seventy-three years of age in 1513, the year of the battle of Flodden. The question will naturally be asked—Would a man of that age lead his clan to battle ? Sir Ewen Cameron of Lochiel was one of the best fighters at the battle of Killiecrankie, yet he was sixty years of age. Lachlan Macquarrie of Ulva, chief of the Macquarries, entered the army in 1778. He was then sixty-two years of age, but he was healthy, active, and perfectly capable of executing any duty of his new profession. He served in the American war, and lived until 1818. Hector MacLean, Eachunn Odhar, was probably as good a man as Lachlan Macquarrie. Why then could he not have taken part in the battle of Flodden ? The old men of 1513 were made of good stuff. They knew nothing about pies or pills, but they knew how to fight.

The descendants of Hector Odhar could have no motive for concealing the fact that his successor was a natural son. Lachlan, his son, was legitimated, and put in possession of the estate. Why then deny that he was a natural son ? The old Highland chiefs were honourable men. If they had natural sons, they were not so mean as to deny that such was the case. They treated such sons in a proper manner ; they loved them as their sons, and took care of them. It was to avenge the death of his natural son that Charles of Drimnin rushed madly back into the fight at Culloden.

So far as known to me, the word "Catanach" means belonging to the Clan-Chattan, and nothing else. The word that means shaggy is "Caiteineach." The word "Catanach" is not in O'Reilly's Irish Dictionary, but the word "Caitineach," curled, napped, is in it. The word "Catanach" is not in the Highland Society's Dictionary, but "Caiteineach," shagged, ruffled as the sea, is in it. The word "Catanach" is not in Macalpine's Dictionary, but "Caiteanach," nappy, shaggy, is in it. The word "Caiteineach" is in Macleod's Dictionary, and is defined as meaning shaggy, rough. But the word "Catanach" is also in Macleod's Dictionary, and is defined as meaning hairy, rough, shaggy ; one of the Clan-Chattan. I am not prepared to say that Dr. Macleod is wrong in explaining the word "Catanach" as

meaning shaggy; all that I can say is that I never heard the word used in that sense, and that I do not think it is used in that sense either in Ireland or Argyllshire. I suspect that if a man had told Neil Macalpine, the Argyllshire lexicographer, that "Catanach" meant shaggy, he would have informed him in fairly emphatic words that it did not.

My reasons for believing that Hector Odhar fought and fell at the battle of Flodden are the following :—

1. The Ardgour MS. states that Hector Odhar succeeded his father, Lachlan Og ; that he was Lieutenant-General to John, Lord of the Isles, at the battle of Bloody Bay, in 1482, and that he was killed at the battle of Flodden in 1513. It also states that he was married to a daughter of MacKintosh, and had Lachlan Catanach by her.

It is certain that Hector Odhar had a son named Lachlan. I consider it equally certain that he was not married to a daughter of the chief of the MacKintoshes. Hector Odhar was a prominent man. Had he married MacKintosh's daughter, the fact would be put on record; but in Alexander MacKintosh Shaw's History of the Clan-Chattan, there is not the slightest reference to such a marriage. At the same time, there can be no reason for doubting that Lachlan Cattanach's mother was a daughter of MacKintosh, or some prominent man among the Clan-Chattan. The fact that he was known as Lachlan Cattanach clearly shows that he was brought up, not in Mull, but among the MacKintoshes.

2. There are two eminent authorities in Highland matters, Gregory and Skene. We are under a very great obligation to both. They may be wrong on some points ; but, as a general rule, they are right. Gregory says that the Lachlan, who was chief of the MacLeans from 1502 to 1527, was Lachlan Cattanach, Lachunn Catanach. *History of the Western Highlands and Islands—Index, page 447.*

3. The Rev. John MacLean, minister of Kilninian, in Mull, must have known the history of his clan. He was licensed to preach in 1702, and died in 1756. In a very fine poem by him, he states that Hector made his body a shield to protect his King from wounds. In a note to this poem, Dr. Hector MacLean, son of Lachlan MacLean of Grulin, says that the Hector referred to is Hector Odhar, who fell at Flodden. The poem will be found in *The Gaelic Bards, from 1715 to 1765*, at page 61.

Hector Odhar was between sixty-three and seventy-three years of age in 1513. Lachlan Cattanach, his son, was in actual possession of Duart. It will perhaps be said that we should, under these circumstances, assume that Lachlan led the MacLeans at Flodden. Hector Odhar had good reasons for leaving Lachlan at home.

1. Lachlan Cattanach was not a popular chief. When he was

a young man, the leading men among the MacLeans of Duart held a meeting at which the propriety of excluding him from the chiefship was considered. His father, of course, was favourable to him, but there was a strong party against him. It is highly probable that those who were against him then continued against him. He was legitimated in 1496, and also put in possession of Duart. These facts, however, would not change the feelings of his followers towards him.

2. Lachlan Cattanach was a cunning man, a politician, a schemer, but he was not a warrior. He was not fitted for leading his clan at Flodden. The man that the MacLeans wanted at their head was not a politician, but a general and fighter.

3. Hector Odhar was a born warrior and a good commander. He was also an exceedingly popular chief. Whilst some of the MacLeans were favourable to Lachlan Cattanach, and others against him, they were all attached to Hector Odhar; they would work for him, fight for him, and follow him anywhere.

It is possible that "Seanachie," author of the History of the MacLeans, published in 1838, is a little too severe upon Lachlan Cattanach; still I think that his account of him is substantially correct. Lachlan was evidently a slippery and crafty man. The author of the sketch of "Ailean nan Sop," which was published in "Cuairtear nan Gleann," in August, 1841, was evidently pretty well acquainted with the history of the MacLeans, but he speaks of Lachlan Cattanach as a *droch dhuine*, a bad man. Lachlan's first wife, Elizabeth Campbell, may have had faults, but it is impossible to excuse Lachlan's conduct in placing her on a rock to be drowned. It is hard to believe that he had a sham funeral for his wife, but from an old Gaelic poem, published in the *Gael* of January, 1873, at page 296, such seems to have been the case. His wife, who procured a divorce from him, was afterwards married to Archibald Campbell of Acha nam-Breac. Lachlan was murdered in Edinburgh by Sir John Campbell of Cader, in 1528. In the Annals of Loch Ce, he is called "Mac Gilla Eain mor Mac Echainn," great MacLean, the son of Hector. To use this statement proves beyond the possibility of doubt that he was the son of Hector Odhar.

THE FIRST FIVE MACLEANS OF ARDGOUR.

Donald, son of Lachlan Bronnach, was the first MacLean of Ardgour. According to the Ardgour MS., Donald's mother was a "daughter of Mac Earchorn, Laird of Kingerloch." In my sketches of the MacLeans, published in the *Celtic Magazine* in 1888, I committed the mistake of stating that she was the daughter of Mac-Mhic-Eachainn, Laird of Kingerloch. Her father was not a MacLean but a MacEachern. The MacEacherns occupied Kingerloch before the MacLeans.—*Skene's Highlanders, Vol. II.*,

p. 122. Donald had four sons—Ewen, his successor ; Neil Ban, Iain Ruadh, and Archibald.

According to the Ardgour MS., Ewen, second Laird of Ardgour, had three sons,—Allan, John, and Hector. He may have had these sons, but it is certain that the name of his eldest son was Lachlan, and it is extremely probably that the name of his second son was Charles. It is quite possible that he had five sons— Lachlan, Charles, Allan, John, and Hector. I suspect, however, that he had no son named Allan.

Lachlan, eldest son of Ewen, was the third MacLean of Ardgour. Gregory says that Lachlan MacEwen MacLean was Laird of Ardgour in 1493. Page 72. Lachlan had a claim to the estate at that time, but his father was still living. We find a remission for all past acts granted to Lachlan MacEwen of Ardgour, in 1517.—*History of the Clan MacLean, pp. 68 and 71.* Lachlan must have died without issue. He was succeeded by his nephew, John, son of Charles.

John was the fourth chieftain of the MacLeans of Ardgour. In an official document of the year 1584, he is called John McCarlych, or John, son of Charles.—*History of the Clan MacLean, p. 83.* In the same document it is stated that he was without lawful heirs. His lands were granted to Hector Mor of Duart.

Allan, fifth of Ardgour, may have been a natural son of John. At the same time he may have been a brother of John. I have no means of determining who he was. He received possession of the estate from Hector Mor of Duart. The fact that the estate was given to Hector of Duart and not to Allan himself, must lead one to suppose that he was a natural son of John. On the other hand, the fact that his second son was called Charles, seems to indicate that Charles was his father's name, and that he was thus a brother of John.

According to the Ardgour MS., Allan was married twice. By his first wife, a daughter of Lochiel, he had one son, Ewen. By his second wife, a daughter of Clanranald, he had two sons, Charles and Lachlan. By a daughter of Marian of Ardnamurchan, with whom he had handfasted for two years, he had also two sons, John of Inverscadell, and one whose name is not given. He had also a natural son who was known as John Gleannach. He had thus six sons, all of whom were in prosperous circumstances. The descendants of these sons called themselves Clann Mhic-Ailein. Allan was succeeded by his son Ewen, Eoghan na h-Iteige.

I have no doubt that the Ardgour MS. gives a correct account of Allan and his sons. But it does not tell us who his father was. It makes no reference at all to John. It thus incorrectly terms Allan the fourth Laird of Ardgour.

49

THE FIRST MACLEAN OF PENNYCROSS.

According to the Ardgour MS., John Dubh of Morvern had four sons, Donald Glas, Allan of Ardtornish, John Garbh, and Charles. Allan of Ardtornish had three sons, Hector, Charles, and Donald Glas. Charles lived at Ardnacross, and had six sons, Allan of Drimnin, Lachlan of Calgary, Allan of Grulin, Donald of Aros, Hector, and Ewen. Lachlan of Calgary had four sons, Donald, Allan, and Peter. Allan of Grulin had three sons, Lachlan of Grulin, Charles of Kilunaig, and John. Charles of Kilunaig had six sons, Allan, Hector, Allan, John, Lachlan, and Alexander. Alexander was a surgeon, and married Una, daughter of Alexander Macgillivray of Pennyghael. This Alexander was the first MacLean of Pennycross.

According to Seanachie's History of the MacLeans, page 344, Prof. MacLean's History, page 309, and Burke's Landed Gentry, John Dubh had Allan of Ardtornish, who had Lachlan of Calgary, who had Allan of Grulin, who had Alexander, first MacLean of Pennycross. Indeed Seanachie's genealogy of the MacLean's of Pennycross, at page 345, is different from the genealogy which he gives at page 340. I think it may be regarded as certain that the genealogy given at page 340 is the correct one. It agrees with the Ardgour MS.

It is extremely desirable that we should have a correct history of the MacLeans. It is to be hoped then that the MacLeans who live in Scotland and have ready access to old books and public documents, will put forth every effort in their power to procure materials for such a history.

It is also desirable to have as full a history as possible, a history containing as many correct genealogies as can be obtained. It must be admitted that there were men among the MacLeans who were not just what men ought to be. But there is no reason to be ashamed of these men; they were no worse than scores of other men who lived in their time. The Clan MacLean, taken as a whole, were as good as any other clan. Some might say that they were better than some other clans. I will not say that; there is nothing to be gained by such an assertion. I do, however, say that the MacLeans were a good clan, a clan that can boast of good poets, good warriors, and good men. Let then those who can trace themselves, link by link, back to "Gilleain na Tuaighe" do so, and let there be no missing links. Paul did not give heed to fables and endless genealogies; at the same time he took a manly and proper interest in the genealogy of his own family, he could tell that he was of the stock of Israel, of the tribe of Benjamin, a Hebrew of the Hebrews.

ALEXANDER MACLEAN SINCLAIR.

Belfast, P. E. Island,
14th Dec., 1892.

50

The following short communication was received from Professor J. P. MacLean Morrison, Whiteside County, Illinois, U.S.A., and it was read before the Association on 9th March :—

There are many obscure things in our history which I trust you will unearth. Among these permit me to mention—

1. There was a Lieut.-Gen. Lachlan MacLean I barely mentioned, not having any further information.

2. A Miss Jessie MacLean warned Prince Charles' forces of the approach of the English just before the battle of Culloden. Reference is made to her in a paper by Wm. Mackay, in "Transactions Gaelic Society of Inverness." Her name should be rescued from oblivion.

3. Lowry Cole MacLean, Bencraig, Seven Oaks, England, sent me the following information concerning Mary Gouin MacLean, fourth daughter of Lachlan, sixth Laird of Muck, who "was a celebrated beauty, mentioned in several books at the beginning of this century. She was born at the beginning of the century, I think in America, as that was her mother's native country. There are still old men alive who remember her when they were boys, when they used to race down all the short cuts in order to have another look at her. Whenever she went to the opera, the people used to fight for a front place to have a look at her. The Emperor of Russia was so struck with her that he offered her a post at the Russian Court, which, needless to say, she did not accept. Her father at the time of his death (1816) was Deputy-Governor of the Tower of London ; and I know nothing of her between that time and about 1825, when she was married at Marylebone Church, Notting Hill, London, to Captain A. Clarke of Coimbu (or Comrie). Soon after his marriage his regiment (the 6th foot) was ordered to Bombay, where he went, accompanied by his wife, and died of apoplexy, in 1827, three months after his only son Andrew's death. The widow then returned to her husband's people, in Edinburgh, where she died 10th April, 1834, leaving a daughter, Hannah, who was living at Oban in 1863, but is since dead (no children). My grandfather, Alex. MacLean of Haremere, who was Mr. Clarke's first cousin, described her as lovely, as was also her sister, Mrs. Henrietta Poore. There was a full-length portrait of Mary Gouin at Oban, but her daughter left it, after her death, to one of the Clarke's. She has numerous neices alive now, one of whom married my uncle, Capt. Henry MacLean ; another Mrs. G. de la Poer Beresford died last month in Australia. Two others are living in Hertfordshire, one of whom has the minature from which the photo. I have was taken." This letter is dated 28th April, 1890. I never received a copy of the photo. although I tried to.

4. In Macleay's ("Rob Roy and Clan Macgregor") account of the abduction of Lady Grange, Margaret MacLean is mentioned

as being indirectly a party to it. Also a MacLean, a parish minister, referring to give Lady Grange the consolations of religion.

5. In Stuart's "Lays of the Deer Forest" (I have parted with my copy), an account is given of the brutal murder of a MacLean, after the battle of Culloden, by the English soldiers.

6. An account of Lachlan MacLean, author of "History of the Celtic Language." He has three nephews, J. W. MacLean, 44 State Street, Chicago; T. K. MacLean, Wichita, Kansas; D. T. Macdonald, Red Jacket, Michigan.

The Gaelic Society of Glasgow should look up the following :—

1. In 1887, Archibald John MacLean, of Pennycross, discovered many crosses, cut in the rock, in the Nun's cave, near Carsaig, Ross of Mull. I had natural size drawings of all these crosses, which I had intended to publish, but were destroyed when I was burned out. A history of the cross, with traditions, description, and illustrations of crosses, would form a very interesting article.

2. On the Garvelloch Isles (near Lochbuie, Isle of Mull) are interesting ecclesiastical ruins. I made drawings of all of them. These were destroyed.

3. On MacLean of Lochbuie's estate, not far from Castle Moy, are the ruins of a druidical circle. I made a drawing and measurements of these. Also destroyed.

All of these subjects are more or less interesting, and I trust that you, or some other enthusiastic Kelt will work out the problems.

THE CLANS AND THEIR CRESTS.

THE MACLEANS.

BY PROFESSOR J. P. MACLEAN.

*Author of " A History of the Clan MacLean ;"
" Fingal's Cave ;" " The Norse Discovery
of America ;" &c., &c.*

COAT-OF-ARMS OF MACLEANS OF DUART.

THE origin of the crest of the MacLeans, which is still used on the coat-of-arms of all the various cadets, is associated with Gilleain, the founder, or father of the Clan, who flourished about the year 1250, and possessed lands in Mull and some of the adjacent islands. He was known as *Gilleain na Tuaigh*, or Gilleain of the battle-axe, on account of his carrying, as his ordinary weapon and constant companion, that implement. The crest consists of a battle-axe between a laural and cypress branch.

There is a tradition, which has always been current among, and invariably believed in by the MacLeans, that upon a certain occasion Gilleain engaged in a stag hunt with other lovers of the chase. For some special reason the party selected the mountain of Beinn t-sheala, which, it would appear, that Gilleain at that time was not familiar with. In the pursuit of game, owing to his eagerness and fleetness of foot, he became separated from his

companions. The mountain having become suddenly covered with mist, he lost his way.

For three days Gilleain wandered about, perplexed, discomfited, and unable to recover his route. So incessantly did he labour that on the fourth day he became exhausted through fatigue, when, under a cranberry bush, after fixing the point of the handle of his battle-axe in the ground, he laid himself down.

When his companions discovered he was missing they set out on a search for him. On the evening of the fourth day, after the day that he was overcome by exhaustion, his friends discovered the head of a battle-axe above a bush, and on drawing near found its owner with his arm encircled around the handle, with his body stretched out on the ground, and in a state of insensibility. Being thus happily rescued he soon was sufficiently recovered, when the whole party returned to their homes. As the battle-axe played an important part in saving the life of Gilleain it was appropriately adopted as the principal part of the crest, and to it the laural and cypress branch were added.

The tartan of all the MacLeans, save that of Lochbuie, is composed of :—½ black, 1½ red, 1 azure, 11 red, 5 green, 1 black, 1½ white, 1 black, ½ yellow, 2 black, 3½ azure, 2 black, ½ yellow, 1 black, 1½ white, 1 black, 5 green, 11 red, 1 azure, 1½ red, 1 black. To this must be added the hunting tartan. On a scale of 5½ inches, given by sixteenths :—3 black, 21 green, 3 black, 3 green, 6 black, 1 white, 6 black, 3 green, 5 black, 1 white, 6 black, 3 green, 3 black, 21 green, 3 black. In this description I commence at the centre of one block and run to the centre of the next, counting first and last as one.

The *Badge* of all the MacLeans, save Lochbuie, is the holly. The *Slogan*—" Bàs na Beatha " (" Death or Life "). *March*— " Caismeachd Eachuinn mhic Ailein nan sop " (" The warning of Hector, son of Allan nan sop "). *Clan Gathering*—" Ceann na Drochaide móire." *Chief's Salute*—
Motto—" Virtue mine honour."

CREST OF THE CLAN MACLEAN ASSOCIATION.

MACLEAN OF DOCHGARROCH.

Motto—"Vincere vel Mori," also "Virtue mine honour."
Present Representative—Allan MacLean, Southsea, England.

Maclean of Ardgour.

ARDGOUR.

Motto—"Altera Merces." *Patronymic*—"Mac Mhic Eóghain."
Present Representative—Alexander John Hew MacLean, Ardgour.

MacLean of Pennycross.

PENNYCROSS.

Motto—" Altera Merces," also " Virtue mine honour." *Present
Representative*—Archibald John MacLean, Pennyghael, Mull.

Maclean of Brolass.

BROLAS.

Motto—" Altera Merces," also "Virtue mine honour." On the
death of Sir Hector MacLean, Bart., in 1750, the Chiefship of the
Clan descended to the House of Brolass. This house did not
assume the coat-of-arms belonging to Mac Ghilleain, or MacLean
of Duart, as it should have done, but retained its own. The
present Chief of the whole Clan is Colonel Sir Fitzroy Donald
MacLean, Bart., 15 Hyde Park Terrace, W., London.

56

Maclaine of Lochbuie.

LOCHBUIE.

Motto—" Vincere vel Mori." *Badge*—Blaeberry. *Patronymic*—
" Mhurchadh Ruadh." The *Tartan* is quite modern, being composed of 34 red, 9 green, 4 blue, 1 yellow, 4 blue, 9 green, on a scale of sixteenths. *Present Representative*—Captain M. G. MacLaine of Lochbuie, Mull.

MacLean of Coll.

COLL.

Motto—" Altera Merces," also " Virtus Durissima Terit." *Clan Gathering*—" Biorlinn Tighearna Cholla." *Patronymic*—" MacIain Abraich." *Present Representative*—

KINGERLOCH.

Patronymic—" Mac Mhic Eachuinn Kingerloch." *Present Representative*—Robert Cutler MacLean, Lynn, Massachusetts, U.S.A.

Morrison, Ill., U.S.A.

BUSINESS MEETING.

Held in Glasgow, 6th April, 1893.

THE first annual business meeting of the Association was held in the Assembly Rooms, Bath Street, on 6th April, 1893, when the chair was occupied by Mr. John MacLean, vice-president, who in the course of a few remarks traced the chief events of the year. The first annual gathering in the Waterloo Rooms—the first great meeting of their Clan since Culloden's fatal day—was, he said, a great success, and as at Culloden their clansmen were led by the chief of their day to do battle for Prince Charlie and the Stewarts, so they in the piping times of peace were presided over by their distinguished and honoured chief, Sir Fitzroy Donald MacLean. That night their chief won golden opinions from the Clan and their friends. Their chief was proud of his Clan, and they were proud of and devoted to their chief. He was a gentleman, a soldier, and all that a Highland chief should be. Long life to him and Lady MacLean, and might the Clan MacLean in Glasgow often have his genial presence as chairman at their annual gatherings. Mr. MacLean referred to the other features of the session, and said that it was to their secretary that the Association owed the the greater part of its success. His abilities, his energies, and his devotion deserved the highest praise, and without him the Associa- would not be what it is. The treasurer and secretary submitted their first annual report on the affairs of the Association, which was unanimously adopted.

Glasgow, the 6th April, 1893.—We, the auditors appointed by the council, have examined the treasurer's and secretary's books, and find them correct.

(*Signed*) JOHN MACLEAN, 60 Mitchell Street, } *Auditors.*
DONALD MACLEAN, 296 Buchanan St.,}

LIST OF MEMBERS.

A. C. H. MacLean, 3 Grosvenor Terrace, Hillhead.
A. H. MacLean, Hughenden Terrace, Kelvinside.
A. J. MacLean, 73 Byres Road, Partick.
Alexander Harry MacLean, 93 Highlander's Umbella, India.
Alexander MacLean, 211 Hospital Street.
Alexander MacLean, Central Agency, St. Enoch Square.
Alexander McLean, Central Police Office, Glasgow.
Alexander MacLean Johnstone, 69 Hyndland Street, Partick.
Alexander MacLean, 26 Gilmour Street, Glasgow.
Alexander MacLean, Coails, Tiree.
Allan Fitzroy MacLean of Pennycross.
Allan MacLean, Crogan, Mull.
Allan MacLean, 62 Alexandria, Alexandria.
Allan MacLean, Kinloch, Pennygeal, Mull.
Allan S. MacLean, 78 George Street, Whiteinch.
Allan Thomas Lockart MacLean, Covington, Thankerton, Lanarkshire.
A. MacLean, 115 Main Street, Bradford, U.S.A.
Andrew MacLean, 4 Princes Gardens, Dowanhill.
Angus MacLean, 17 George Street, Westminster.
Angus MacLean, Scrap, Tarbert, Harris.
Angus MacLean, 405 St. Vincent Street, Glasgow.
Angus MacLean, 22 Gardner Street, Partick.
Angus MacLean, 17 Cleaveland Street, Glasgow.
Archibald A. MacLean, Hughenden Terrace, Kelvinside.
Archibald MacLaine, 56 Paterson Street.
Archibald MacLean, 149 Renfrew Street, Glasgow.
Archibald MacLean, 2 Spring Place, Partick.
C. A. MacLean, Solicitor, Wigton.
Captain Donald MacLean, 52 Pollok Street, Glasgow.
Captain Kenneth MacLean, Yacht Satellete.
Charles Alexander MacLean of Pennycross.
Charles H. MacLean, Fintry, Aberdeenshire.
Charles MacLean, Withcot Farm, Oakham.
Charles MacLean, Railway Tavern, Bridge of Weir.
Charles MacLean, 3 Cadzow Street, Glasgow.
C. J. MacLean, 3 Grosvenor Terrace, Hillhead.
Colin MacLean, Mid Dana, Knapdale, Argyll.
Col. Sir Fitzroy Donald MacLean, Bart.
Daniel MacLean, 119 George Street, Glasgow.
Donald MacLean, 189 Paisley Road, West.

60

Donald MacLean, 37 North Albion Street.
Donald MacLean, 40 South Portland Street.
Donald MacLean, 8 Whitefield Road,{Govan.
Donald MacLean, 61 Kersland Street, Hillhead.
Donald MacLean, 466 New City Road.
Donald MacLean, 478 Pollokshaws Road.
Donald MacLean, 26 Cornwall Street, Govan.
Donald MacLean, 296 Buchanan Street, Glasgow.
Donald MacLean, 15 M'Lean Street, Plantation.
Donald MacLean, The Crofts, Lochbuie, Mull.
Donald MacLean, Argyle Terrace, Tobermory.
Donald MacLean, 466 New City Road.   -
Donald MacLean, 40 South Portland Street.
Dr. MacLean, Paisley Road, Glasgow.
Dr. MacLean, Swindon House, Swindon.
Dr. MacLean, Greek Street, Stockport.
Dugald MacLean, — South Portland Street.
Duncan MacLean, 40 South Portland Street.
Duncan MacLean, 40 Edmund Street, Glasgow.
Duncan MacLean, Balevulin, Pennygeal, Mull.
Duncan MacLean, 13 Alexander Grove, Manchester.
Duncan MacLean, 20 Moray Place, Strathbungo.
Duncan MacLean, Dalmuir.
Ewen MacLean, Merchant, Lochmaddy.
Ewen MacLean, 112 Church Street, Inverness.
Ex-Provost MacLean, Govan.
Fred. Lachlan McLean, 68 St. Vincent Crescent.
Gilliane MacLaine, Tiroran, Mull.
Hamish MacLean, 40 Dunmore Street, Glasgow.
Hector Fitzroy MacLean.
Hector MacLean, 166 Holm Street, Glasgow.
Hector MacLean, Blantyre Street, Glasgow.
Hector MacLean, 13 Wellshot Terrace.
Hector MacLean, 3 Cadzow Street, Glasgow.
Henry Hector MacLean, 110 Eaglesham Street, Glasgow.
Herbert MacLean, 296 Buchanan Street, Glasgow.
Hope MacLean, 3 Grosvenor Terrace, Hillhead.
Hugh MacLean, 26 M'Kinlay Street, Glasgow.
J. A. MacLean, Union Bank, Forfar.
James MacLean, Breaknock Road, London.
James MacLean, Bellsaugh Cottage, Temple.
James MacLean, Jun., Bellsaugh Cottage, Temple.
James MacLean, 28 Norfolk Street, Glasgow.
James MacLean, Lithographer, 57 West Nile Street.
James MacLean, 8 Woodlands Road, Glasgow.
James MacLean, 2 Victoria Place, Clydebank.
James MacLean, 98 Shamrock Street, Glasgow.

61

John MacLean, 60 Mitchell Street.
John MacLean, 73 Byres Road, Partick.
John MacLean, 93 West Regent Street.
John MacLean, Rokeby Terrace, Hillhead.
John MacLean, 86 Wilson Street, Glasgow.
John MacLean, 35 Rose Street, Garnethill.
John MacLean, Baraland, N. Uist.
John MacLean, Glendaruel Cottage, Dunoon.
John MacLean, Regworth, England.
John MacLean, 9 Moir Street, Glasgow.
John MacLean, 228 Paisley Road.
John MacLean, 114 West Nile Street, Glasgow.
John MacLean, Builder, Ardrossan.
John MacLean, 4 Buchanan Street, Partick.
John MacLean, Duke Street, Glasgow.
John MacLean, 125 North Street, Glasgow.
John MacLean, 73 North Street, Glasgow.
John MacLean, Kinloch, Pennygeal, Mull.
John MacLean, Mason, Bredalbane Street, Tobermory.
John MacLean, Tiroran, Mull.
John MacLean, Inns Salen, Mull.
John MacLean, Portree, Skye.
John MacLean, Hughenden Terrace, Kelvinside.
John MacLean, 113 Kent Road, Glasgow.
John MacLean, 83 Dumbarton Road.
John MacLean, Postmaster, Helensburgh.
John MacLean, 40 York Place, Perth.
John MacLean Johnstone, 28 Overnewton Place, Glasgow.
John Watson McLean, 68 St. Vincent Crescent.
Kenneth MacLean, Merchant, Lochmaddy.
Kenneth MacLean, 1 Carlisle Terrace, Kelvinside.
Lachlan McLean, 68 St. Vincent Crescent.
Lachlan MacLean, 31 Alma Street, Govan.
Lachlan MacLean, 56 Paterson Street, Glasgow.
Lachlan MacLean, Gardner Street, Partick.
Lachlan MacLean, 261 Stirling Road, Glasgow.
Lachlan Maclean, Coails, Tiree.
Lachlan MacLean, Balevulin, Pennygeal, Mull.
Lachlan MacLean, 29 North Woodside Road.
MacLean Edgar, Craigmore Terrace, Partick.
MacLean of Ardgour.
MacLean of Guilean.
MacLean of Pennycross.
MacLean of Torloisk.
Magnus MacLean, M.A., 8 St. Albans Terrace.
Malcolm MacLean, Kirkpool, Tiree.
Malcolm MacLean, Kinloch, Pennygeal, Mull.

62

Malcolm MacLean, 8 Caledonia Place, Clydebank.
Malcolm MacLean, 172 Dumbarton Road, Glasgow.
Matthew MacLean, Lock-keeper, Caledonian Canal.
Murdo MacLean, Loch Broom, Ross-shire.
Neil MacLaine, 2 Ruthland Crescent, Paisley Road.
Neil MacLean, 474 Cathcart Road.
Neil MacLean, 47 Fleming Street, Govan.
Neil MacLean, 27 Raeberry Street.
Neil MacLean, Mid Dana, Knapdale, Argyll.
Neil MacLean, 7 Gardner Street, Partick.
Neil MacLean, Coails, Tiree.
Neil MacLean, 7 Royal Bank Place, Glasgow.
Neil MacLean, Balevulin, Pennygeal, Mull.
Norman Henry MacLean of Pennycross.
Peter MacLean, Solicitor, Lochmaddy.
Peter MacLean, Forester, Invergarry.
Peter MacLean Robertson, Bath Hotel, Glasgow.
Peter MacLean, 174 New City Road.
Peter MacLean, 31 Elderslie Street.
Peter MacLean Paul, 1 Hayburn Terrace, Partick.
Provost MacLean, Gowanlea, Largs.
R. A. MacLean, 163 Crown Street, Glasgow.
Rev. A. MacLean Sinclair, Prince Edward Island, Canada.
Rev. Dr. MacLean, 189 Hill Street, Garnethill.
Rev. F. MacLean, Banff.
Rev. J. T. MacLean, Govan.
R. MacLean MacLean, Elliot Hill, Kent.
Robert MacLean, 31 Cadogan Street.
Robert MacLean, Cumbernauld Road.
Robert MacLean, 151 Renfrew Street, Glasgow.
Robert K. MacLean, Hughenden Terrace, Kelvinside.
Roderick MacLean, 34 Clarendon Street, Partick.
Sir Andrew MacLean, Partick.
Spencer B. MacLean, 8 Smith Street, Hillhead.
The Rev. Arthur John MacLean, Dean of Argyll and the Isles.
Thomas MacLean, Kinloch, Pennygeal, Mull.
Thomas MacLean, Hotel Keeper, Neither Lochaber Hotel.
Thomas MacLean, Banker, Alexandria.
Vallance W. MacLean, 165 Govan Street, Glasgow.
Walter MacLean, Hampton Court Terrace, Glasgow.
William J. MacLean, Chapiefield, Barrhead.
William MacLean Homan, 6 Buckingham Terrace.
William MacLean, 188 West Regent Street.
William MacLean, 10 Somerset Place.
William MacLean, 110 King Street, Govan.
William MacLean, Mishnish Hotel, Tobermory.
William MacLean, C.A., 98 West George Street, Glasgow.

63

William MacLean, 345 St. Vincent Street, Glasgow.
William MacLean, 3 Grosvenor Terrace, Hillhead.
William Norman MacLean, Hughenden Terrace, Kelvinside.

———

Baroness De Pallandt MacLean, London.
Dowager Mrs. MacLean of Pennycross.
Honrd. Mrs. Ralph W. Melville, N. Maidstone.
Lady MacLean, Moreton Hall, England.
Miss Annie Jane MacLean, Kilberry, Argyllshire.
Miss Annie MacLaine, 56 Paterson Street.
Miss Annie MacLean, 73 Byres Road, Partick.
Miss Annie MacLean, Aird, Mull.
Miss Bella MacLaine, 2 Ruthland Crescent.
Miss Catherine MacLean, 8 Princess Terrace, Glasgow.
Miss Catherine MacLean, Kinloch, Mull.
Miss Christina MacLean, 26 Bellhaven Terrace, Glasgow.
Miss Christina MacLean, Coails Cottage, Tyree.
Miss C. MacLean, 113 Inverness Terrace, London.
Miss Flora MacLean, 70 West Street, Govan.
Miss Helena G. McLean, 68 St. Vincent Crescent, Glasgow.
Miss Henrietta MacLaine, Scoble, Mull.
Miss Jane W. MacLean, Hughenden Terrace.
Miss Jessie MacLean, 58 Park Road Glasgow.
Miss Lizzie MacLean, 24 Carmichael Street, Govan.
Miss MacLean of Pennycross.
Miss MacLean, 188 West Regent Street, Glasgow.
Miss MacLean, 113 Hyde Park Terrace, London.
Miss Maggie MacLean, 58 Park Road, Glasgow.
Miss Maggie S. W. McLean, 68 St. Vincent Crescent, Glasgow.
Miss Marion MacLaine, 2 Rutland Crescent.
Miss Mary Flora MacLean, University Avenue, Glasgow.
Miss Mary Gardner MacLean, Cartdale House, Langside.
Miss Mary MacLean, 77 Dumbarton Road, Partick.
Miss Mary S. McLean, 68 St. Vincent Crescent, Glasgow.
Miss Mina MacLean, Regs. Office, Shamrock Street.
Miss Nellie S. MacLean, 3 Grosvenor Crescent, Hillhead.
Mrs. A. H. MacLean, Hughenden Terrace.
Mrs. Anderson, 57 Wharton Road, W., Kensington Park, London.
Mrs. Andrew MacLean, 4 Princes Gardens, Hillhead.
Mrs. Brodie, Ethel Terrace, Mount Florida.
Mrs. C. J. MacLean, 3 Grosvenor Crescent, Hillhead.
Mrs. Donald MacLean, 40 South Portland Street.
Miss E. F. N. MacLean, Redcliff House, Folkestone.
Mrs. Elizabeth MacLean Robertson, Bath Hotel, Glasgow.
Mrs. Hall, Elmbank, Kilmarnock.
Mrs. Helen MacLean, Menish Hotel, Tobermory.
Mrs. Homan, Norway.

OFFICERS.

WILLIAM A. MCLEAN, President.

J. P. MACLEAN, Corresponding Secretary.

S P MACLEAN, Recording Secretary

ARTHUR A MACLEAN, Treasurer

COMMITTEE OF ARRANGEMENTS.

JAMES A MCLANE,

THOMAS A MACLEAN,

JOHN W MCLEAN,

ARCHIBALD B MCLEAN, Jr.

JOHN P MACLEAN

VICE-PRESIDENTS.

Geo. H. McLean,	New York.	Dr. John McLean,	Pullman, Ill
Dr. Thos. Neil. McLean,	Elizabeth, N. J.	Dr. J. T. McLean,	New Philadelphia, O.
Rev. Calvin B. McLean,	Simsbury, Conn.	James A. McLean,	Hamilton, O.
Frank E. McLean,	Union City, Pa.	R. B. McLean,	Nashville, Tenn.
Archibald McLean,	Bradford, Pa.	Alex. McLean,	Richmond, Va.
Barton W. McLean,	Pittsburgh, Pa.	Prof. Joseph McLean,	Charlotte, N. C.
S. Adelbert McLean,	Bay City, Mich.	A. M. McLean,	Lamberton, N. C.
R. E. McLean,	Escanaba, Mich.	Geo. C. McClean,	Springfield, Mass.
Dr. Rob't A. McLean,	San Francisco, Cal.	Chas. A. McLane,	Laredo, Tex.
J. O. Maclean,	Los Angeles, Cal.	H. H. McLane,	San Antonio, Tex.
Wm. B. Maclean,	Toronto, Ont.	Chas. G. Maclean,	Pensacola, Fla.
Jas. H. McLean,	Brantford, Ont.	L. N. McLean,	Cheyenne Falls, Col.
W. Hector McLean,	Crinan, Ont.	H. Z. McLain,	Crawfordsville, Ind.
J. S. McLain,	Minneapolis, Minn.	Hugh H. McLean,	St John, N. B.
Dr. John McLean,	Morehead, Minn.	Hector MacLean,	Bridgeton, N. S.
Dr. J. D. McLean,	Spokane, Wash.	Hon. Emelin McLain,	Iowa City, Iowa.
A. F. McLean,	Tacoma, Wash.		

RECEPTION COMMITTEE.

Geo. C. McLean,	Janesville, Wis.	Arthur O. McLain,	Chicago.
Archibald Maclean,	Rockford, Ill.	A. B. McLean, Sr.,	Chicago.
Dr. John McLean,	Pullman, Ill	Hon. Alex. McLean,	Macomb, Ill.
Dr. Donald Maclean,	Detroit, Mich.	Dr. R. A. McLean,	San Francisco, Cal.
Prof. J. P. MacLean,	Greenville, Ohio.	Hon. W.F.Maclean,M.P.	Toronto, Ont.

1082.   1893.

The Chicago

Association Clan Maclean

requests the presence of yourself and

ladies at the Banquet

to be given in honor of their Chief,

Sir Fitzroy Donald Maclean, Bart.,

at the Auditorium,

~~Thursday~~
Friday Evening, June Fifteenth;

eighteen hundred and ninety-three,

Mrs. James McLean, Pellsaugh Cottage, Temple.

Mrs. James MacLean, 215 Holm Street.

Mrs. Jessie MacLean Galbraith, 188 West Regent Street.

Mrs. John MacLean, 73 Byres Road, Partick.

Mrs. John MacLean, 339 Dumbarton Road.

Mrs. Lachlan McLean, 68 St. Vincent Crescent, Glasgow.

Mrs. MacGavin, Windsor Crescent, Mount Florida.

Mrs. MacLean, 113 Hyde Park Terrace, London.

Mrs. MacLean, Bellahouston Terrace, Ibrox.

Mrs. MacLean Edgar, 9 Craigmore Terrace, Partick.

Mrs. MacLean of Pennycross.

Mrs. Magnus MacLean, 8 St. Albans Terrace.

Miss Mary MacLean, Hughenden Terrace.

Mrs. Mary T. D. MacLean, Windsor Hotel, Glasgow.

Mrs. Mina Crossie MacLean, Greek Street, Stockport.

Mrs. Neil MacLaine, 2 Ruthland Crescent, Paisley Road.

Mrs. Neil MacLean, 24 Kinning Street.

Mrs. Paton, 94 Edith Road, Kensington, London.

Mrs. Phillips, 21 Addison Gardens, K., London.

Mrs. Thomas L. MacLean, Covington Thankerton, Lanarkshire.

Mrs. W. E. Garnett Bolfield, Bishop Castle, Shropshire.

Mrs. Western, 33 Palace Gardens, Kensington, London.

The Lady Hood of Avalon.

www.ingramcontent.com/pod-product-compliance
Lightning Source LLC
Chambersburg PA
CBHW060245030726
47493CB00025B/2340